DRAGON THIRST

Mythos

T.B. PHILLIPS

Books by T.B. Phillips

Dragon Thirst
Legends (September 2023)
Mythos (September 2023)

Andalon Saga

Andalon Origins
Andalon Project (April 2022)
Andalon Paradox (April 2023)
Andalon Prophecies (Expected Winter 2023)

Dreamers of Andalon
Andalon Awakens (June 2019)
Andalon Arises (July 2020)
Andalon Attacks (December 2020)

Children of Andalon
Andalon Legacy (September 2022)

Corrupted Realms
Orphan Knight (July 2023)
Wailing Tempest (May 2021)
Howling Shadow (September 2021)

Chilling Tales
Ferryman (October 2022)

Corrupted Realms
Orphan Knight (July 2023)
Wailing Tempest (April 2021)
Howling Shadow (September 2021)

Dragon Thirst: Mythos

In the beginning the world belonged to mankind—fledgling and barely emerged from wilderness. The arrival of divine messengers, harbingers sent to forge a world in which humans would thrive, nearly sped their downfall instead. Arriving with grace but blinded by arrogance, the divine blazed a prosperous path benefiting themselves. But soon these Keryx found their charges alluring, the simplistic beauty of human form fanned insatiable desire.

The resulting offspring, known as Titans or Nephilim, are recounted separately by every culture's legends. They ruled over earth and treated mankind as simple animals. Man wrote these creatures into their story as gods—they live today in mythos.

This is the story of those ancient and divine bloodlines, how they existed alongside simple humans, steering their lives while committed to the total destruction of rivals. It tells of variants who emerged as mythological heroes and foes.

The bloodlines of these Keryx war to this day...

Choose your form...

Part I

Chapter One

Two Years Ago

Trapped. She knew the feeling but not quite from where.

Pitch blackness wrapped this woman tightly and every muscle cramped from lack of use. Whatever this prison may be, it squeezed panic into her gasping lungs. These burned from the effort, angry and raw as if only just used.

Getting out mattered more than breathing.

She clawed the walls with sharp nails, hard like granite as if grown especially for this task of escape. The need for freedom drove her as they scratched and dug at the hard shell.

Shell? Blinded by darkness she may as well be sealed inside an egg.

A single finger finally broke through followed by a desperate hand shoved through to outside. The crackling outer layer crumbled and she ripped it apart until arms, shoulders, head and torso could wriggle out. She fell in a heap against a cold, rocky floor, her hands wet and slimy. Only soft paper-thin coatings remained where talons had ripped free.

Exhausted, she deeply breathed musty air. She lay there until sleep proved overpowering. That slumber brought awful dreams. Far off in her mind the young woman shivered against dreadful cold. Winter would arrive after drenching rain turned fully to ice and snow. The meager stack of wood ran low, and she turned to a young boy and asked him to gather more.

"Get it yourself," he snapped, pressing his body against the hearth, hogging what little warmth it provided. "You're not Mother!"

"No," she replied, grabbing and twisting his ear while pulling him to his feet, "but Father left *me* in charge!" She added a shove for good measure.

The boy pulled on his ridiculously large boots, those left behind by Father when he left to fight the war. No man in their village was spared conscription, not when every able-bodied soldier was needed. It mattered not if those soldiers were merely farmers like him. They all bled and died the same. After pulling on a jacket and furry hat, the boy snarled as he pushed past his sister.

"Get enough for several weeks," she added. "Snow will fall soon, making it harder to gather."

"*Mother* would have made you go with me," he muttered. The door slammed shut behind him.

Mother had also gone away but no one knew why, not even Father. She left her family without warning, leaving only memories and remembered stories of heroes and legends long passed. The little brother clung to those myths, yearning for dragons and their bonded riders to come rescue them from boredom. His sister wanted only to escape the poverty and hunger they faced, wishing their parents had not abandoned them to this drafty cabin in the woods.

She awoke, shivering against the stone.

Something scratched her eyes and she blinked, careful not to rub too hard. Her fingers pulled away what felt like scabs. To her surprise, sight returned the moment they ripped free.

Soft light emanated from the rocks all around. Though faint, that glow revealed her prison had indeed been an egg. Next to the cracked and broken pieces of shell she found another fully intact. A large skeleton encircled the room, it may have once belonged to a dragon, if such things existed.

Fear filled the girl followed by worry, her eyes focusing on the second egg. *Who or what would emerge?* she wondered.

The remains of an ancient satchel sat nearby, brittle and torn. When she touched it the outer layer crumbled into dust. Inside she found what appeared to be a curved piece of bone. If it had not been so large she would have guessed it a tooth. She eyed the large skull looming nearby and judged it a perfect fit. Anything else of value within the satchel had long ago rotted. She tossed the tooth aside and left, desperate for food and drink and to be away from this cavern.

She fumbled around in darkness, wishing for more of the glowing rocks to guide her. Without their light she moved slowly, frantically feeling along walls. Her biggest fear was that the ground would fall away beneath her bare feet, so she inched them carefully along the barren rock, feeling for firmness ahead.

After what must have been several hours, she heard voices. Not long after, she also saw bright lights up ahead, sweeping the walls, floor, and ceiling of a twisting tunnel. Panic filled the woman who looked back the way she had come. Too many passages waited behind her. There was no way to know from which she had emerged.

The voices grew closer, a mixture of women and men laughing and conversing in some foreign tongue. Some of their words held strange familiarity but were lost upon her ears. Pressing her body against the rocks, she hid her nakedness and shivered against the cold.

Sudden gasps announced the people had seen her, and their lights pointed directly in her direction.

"Wait," one of the women said to the others, "she looks afraid."

Those words meant nothing to the woman's ears.

"We won't hurt you," the woman said again. "What's your name?" Again, the language lost its meaning.

The young woman looked up at the stranger dressed in odd clothing. She wore pants like a man and a shirt with Greek letters across its front. *Chi Omega*, they read. Her hand held a metal torch and a satchel hung by two straps on her back. She wore a helmet atop her head but not at all like the Roman soldiers this woman remembered.

"*Me solum relinquatis,*" she begged, in case they were Roman after all.

"Is that Spanish?" one of the men asked.

"Latin," the other girl explained, a word right away recognized by the woman. "I'll ask her if she's lost. Um... *Peristi?*" the girl asked.

The young woman, naked and afraid in the cave, nodded her head vigorously. "*Ita*," she said. "*Ita sum!*"

"Yes, she is!" the second girl translated. To one of the young men she commanded, "Take off your sweatshirt, she's freezing!" The man set down his satchel then removed his outer garment. His undershirt read *Zeta Beta Tau*. "We've got to get her to Professor Redder," the girl suggested. "My Latin isn't very good and his is better." She gently held out the boy's outer garment and begged, "*Gerunt hoc. Nos te in domum suam.* Where is your home?"

Domus, the young woman thought, eagerly pulling the large tunic over her head, *I can't remember where home is!*

She allowed this girl to help her to her feet, pulled on the tunic, and followed as they led her to the surface. Their metal torches bobbed the entire way, shining brighter than any light she had ever seen besides daylight. Outside, a cold rain fell just like in her dream, the one of that angry boy and the cabin in the woods. Winter clung to that freezing rain, lingering just a few days away.

They brought her to a man, older than the others but youthful in his own right. He would have been around Father's age when he went away for war. Hair had long ago fled from this man's head, and he wore what little he had in a bushy mustache. He wore the same blue pants of the others and a tunic of similar design. His was emblazoned with an orange bull with wide horns.

The younger men spoke in low voices to their leader, with heads held close in congress. The girls led the young woman to a colorful tent and found pants and a heavier coat to wear. Their packs were nothing like she had ever seen, with straps and odd clasps to keep them secure.

These strangers also carried flat objects in their hands. One side of these glowed brightly, almost as brightly as their torches. *What devilry is this?* the young woman wondered. She thought she glimpsed an image of one of the girls on the face of one device.

"Professor Redder," one of the girls called out in their strange language, holding up her device. "Should I call the police?"

"Not yet," the older man warned. "I first want to verify she's indeed speaking Latin. If she is, they'll need a translator. I'd be the first to get her story either way, and I don't want to wait." He walked over with a smile both that she found warm and inviting. "*Latin tibi placet?*" he asked.

"*Gallicus,*" she replied matter of fact.

"I'll be damned," he whispered.

"What did she say?" one of the girls demanded.

"She said she prefers to speak Gaulish."

"What's wrong with that? Do you speak it?" one of the young men asked.

"I can, but mostly only ever *read* it. But that's not the problem. Gaulish hasn't been spoken since the sixth century. As a written language it was replaced by Latin in the first century B.C." He cleared his throat and asked in his best attempt at her language, "What is your name?"

"I don't remember," she admitted.

"How did you get here? Do you remember that?"

She almost told him, but realized no one would believe she hatched from an egg, not any more than she herself did. "I woke up in there," she lied.

"Hmm," the older man frowned.

"What?" one of the girls asked.

"She claims not to remember anything, and says she just woke up in the cave." He tapped his chest. "I am Vince," he introduced himself. "Vincent Redder. I am a professor at the university and these are my students."

"Where are we?" the young woman asked.

"We're an hour outside of Austin, Texas, ma'am," he said with a smile. "And I have to say you're very lucky to have come across the one man in the state who speaks Gaulish."

The young woman frowned. She had never heard of a place called Texas.

"Where are you from?" he asked.

"Cardac," she replied to her own surprise. Mention of the name brought forth an odd sensation. All at once memories flooded forth, some she recognized as her own and others she found too strange to have been real. One name came forward, ahead of many others. "Briaca," she whispered, realizing the name indeed belonged to her. Many more names rushed forth, attached to horrific creatures with broad wings and sharp teeth lusting after sanguis.

Sanguis, she remembered, *did not necessarily mean blood.*

"Briaca?" Vince asked. "Is that your name?"

She nodded. Her vision clouded, fading in and out as her heart thumped out of rhythm.

"Briaca, are you okay?"

The world around the young woman swayed and then turned black.

Chapter Two

Cardac, Helvetia 450 A.D.

Briaca watched through the window, peering between shutters and careful not to let in the icy rain. It pelted the forested valley and coated everything with its misery. She and her brother had already endured three days of this wetness, and the thatch roofing dripped steadily onto the dirt floor below. She let out a sigh. Her village, the people of Cardac, had been through so much—poverty, plague, and, most recently, war had taken away the men.

She squinted, trying to get a glimpse of Kado. He had been gone long enough to gather enough wood to last all winter but no doubt had found a dry spot to wait out the storm. He would regret that soon, when the rain turned to ice and eventually snow.

Briaca pulled the shutter tight and returned to the hearth. A heavy pot hung over the fire, filled with mostly broth and what little remained of their meat. She and Kado would have to hunt again soon, since Lars took all their livestock during his last visit to Cardac.

"I might as *well* be his mother," she muttered, their argument still lingering in her thoughts. What had that woman ever done for either of them besides tell stories too fanciful to believe? She taught her children to believe in dragons and of men riding atop the legendary aerouants.

Tears welled and a sob caught in her throat. Anger pushed it down. Briaca hated their mother for leaving, walking out in the middle of the night and leaving her children and husband without warning. Father had borne the brunt of it, crying himself softly to sleep not knowing his children could hear.

But Briaca had heard, she recognized the sound because she had done the same.

She hated that she and Kado always fought, but the boy never obeyed unless she spoke firmly and with authority. He was a dreamer, wasting his waking moments believing dragons would save them. This interfered with his chores. She had two more summers to put up with him, then he would be old enough to apprentice in the village. After that she would be free to find a husband and marry. *But not until then,* she thought with more than a touch of resentment.

Briaca had already passed the age of maturity but, even if there were men young enough in Cardac for her to marry, none would want a wife burdened with raising a younger sibling.

Though there were plenty of women in Cardac with whom to seek counsel, she avoided them all. They only cried and worried over their men or spoke with scathing resentment over Lars and his thugs. Each time the warlord paid the village a visit they lost a little more. Worse, some of the women disappeared the last time he left. Everyone lived in fear of the man.

Only Argant, the village storyteller, provided Briaca with welcomed conversation. He popped in now and again to visit, bringing small game for the stew. He always told a story or two after dinner. After that he would leave Briaca to her loneliness and Kado to his wild dreams of adventure.

"I've lived through many wars," the old man told her during his last visit, "and they never last forever. Your father and the other men will return home eventually."

"And if he doesn't?" she had asked him.

He only shrugged. "Whether he does or doesn't, you'll have to make your own way in the world. Until then, do your best to raise your brother with love. Fuel his spirit with the stories your mother taught you."

"Those make him restless," she had argued, "and he does less of his chores the more his mind wanders after adventure."

Argant had shrugged again. "Then perhaps all he needs is adventure."

At that Briaca had laughed, then hurried the old man along his way. That had been several months before.

The ringing of bells drew her to the door. The village rang with alarm, and shouts echoed along with the clanging of warning. She pulled the door open and stepped outside. Cold wind and rain sent a shiver down her spine, and she wrapped a wool cloak around her shoulders. It was thin and riddled with moth holes but was the warmest garment she owned.

Kado was running toward the house, clutching Father's axe in one hand and dragging a sled with his other. He had only gathered a few days' worth of firewood, and some of it spilled as he skidded to a halt. His wide eyes betrayed fear.

"What's happening?" she demanded.

"I'm not sure." He let go of the sled and held up Father's axe. With weapon aloft he foolishly offered, "Stay here and I'll go find out."

She reached quickly, grabbing the long handle and wrenching the tool away. She held it firmly out of his reach. "No," she said with that air of authority he hated, "you will go inside." She drilled a stare into him, forcing him to comply. "You'd get yourself killed just for holding this thing! What if it's Lars? He'll gut you for sport!"

For a brief moment Kado stood with back straight, summoning enough courage as if intending to challenge her command. But then he sighed and visibly deflated. With slackened shoulders he strode through the open door.

With a heavy push Briaca let it slam behind him. *He's safer in here,* she thought, then worried he wouldn't be. She hurried down the road, glancing several times over her shoulder at the cabin and its stream of smoke swirling from the chimney. She hiked up her skirts to run faster as muddy rain splashed against her bare legs. She would have shivered had her heart not pumped fast from fear. The town was three furlongs away and she reached it in a few minutes.

She skidded to a halt, panting with hands on knees as she caught her breath. Lifting her head, she looked around, watching as mercenaries kicked open doors, dragging villagers out into the rain. Briaca froze with panic when she realized why.

Muddy and shivering, they were sorted by gender and age. Women of childbearing years were taken to the meeting lodge, shoved inside with those separated from their children. The oldest, the grandmothers and aged widows, were shoved into carts which were no more than cages on wheels drawn behind horses. The youngest children and adolescent girls were locked with them, while the older boys were led to another. The elderly men were pushed into the temple.

Lars' sell swords did not drive these wagons. Heralded soldiers sat atop each. These were King Chilperic's men but sat beside those loyal to Lord Eduard, leader over Cardac.

They're taking the younger boys to war! she realized, lingering just long enough to watch the warlord emerge from a home.

Lars was a large man, tall, well-muscled and properly fed. He dressed as a nobleman despite his low birth was well known. His long, red hair clung to his shoulders as he turned emerald eyes toward Briaca. They smiled devilishly as she quickly turned and fled the way she had come. She never looked back to see if she was followed, knowing the man and his goons surely would.

She reached the cabin in less time than it took to first reach the village, slamming her body against the door and pushing it open with her weight. Cold wind and rain followed her inside, where she watched Kado jump with fright. He spun around, wielding a pathetic stick and waving it around like a sword. The tip, glowing red where he had poked the flames, broke off, falling to the dirt floor. With a panicked step he stomped it out. He looked up at his sister, no doubt afraid she would be angry he had played with fire, but she had no time for such foolishness. All she cared about was getting her brother to safety and out of reach of Lars.

"Pack a satchel," she commanded, pushing the door closed, her voice a mixture of fear and irritation.

"What happened?" Kado demanded, standing where he was instead of doing as told. With no time to waste, she packed it for him.

"No time to explain," she insisted, tossing bread and dried meats into a sack. "You have to leave *now!*"

"Where shall we go?" the boy questioned, his earlier defiance had waned, replaced by fear. He put down the stick and grabbed Father's boots from the hearth, pulling them on.

"You're going alone," she insisted, "but only for a night or two. Lars is in the village, and he's looking for more boys for Lord Eduard's army. You're the oldest now, and they're coming this way."

"I can't go alone," he pleaded. "Come with me!"

Briaca wanted to do just that, to run for the hills and escape the warlord's reach, but she stubbornly held out the sack of food and a bloated waterskin.

"I can't," Kado whispered, tears welling up and choking off whatever convincing he could say to change her mind.

"Run for the hills, find old man Argant, and hide out with him. I will come for you after Lars has gone and it's safe to return," she promised.

Kado wrapped Briaca in a tight hug, gripping her fearfully. With no other option but obedience, he grabbed the satchel and fled into the storm.

She watched her brother from the open door, praying to the gods he would reach Argant's cave unseen. If anything happened to her brother she would never forgive herself. She sent another prayer for Father, begging the gods to return him safely and soon. They could *keep* Mother.

Once she had lost sight of him for several minutes, she stepped inside and pushed shut the door. A large boot appeared, wedging it open. A heavy shoulder shoved it aside, sending her flying backward against the wall. Dazed, she slumped to the floor.

Strong arms grabbed and dragged Briaca outside by her legs, her mouth trying to scream but managing only gurgles and spats as her face splashed through puddles. Once they rolled her onto her back, she screamed at her attackers, "Get your hands off of me!"

The nearest smiled down, leaning over to threaten some lewd promise. She responded with a kick to his knee, drawing forth a grunt. Leaping to her feet, she tried to run, but three others grabbed and held her tight. A fourth stood inside her open door. A scrawny man with a crooked nose smiled, he dashed jar after jar of food stores against the wall.

"You won't be needing these," he promised, "not as a slave."

"Is that what you're doing?" she demanded. "Lars gets slaves and Lord Eduard gets boys to aid King Chilperic's war?"

"The term is *serf*, actually," Crooked Nose corrected himself, "essentially slaves to the land. But you're pretty, maybe he'll keep you in his fortress as a chamber wench."

"I'd rather kill myself," she swore, stomping hard on the ankle of the man to her right. He loosened his grasp just as Crooked Nose lunged. Briaca stepped aside, bringing her foot up hard to meet his groin. His knees buckled and he collapsed, his spindly frame too encumbered with pain. A howling moan announced it would be some time before he could stand.

She gave him another kick for good measure.

One of the others pulled out a club, swinging it and catching her too off-balance to move out of the way. It struck the small of her back, knocking the air from her lungs. She crumbled, unable to cry out.

The thugs quickly bound her hands and secured a hood over her head. Dazed, she could no longer struggle as they dragged her off. She felt her body being lifted high into the air then landed hard on a wooden slab, the back of their wagon, no doubt, and lay there listening as the warlord arrived.

"Four of you against one girl, and you imbeciles let her get the best of you?" Lars asked with a laugh.

"She fights like an Amazon!" Crooked Nose complained, then chuckled. "Where's the boy? Surely you didn't let *him* best *you*!"

"He's surely dead," Lars grumbled.

Briaca felt her heart skip a beat, and her stomach twisted with worry.

"Surely, but you're not certain?" Crooked Nose accused.

"Dead enough, and worthless in trade. An old man intervened. Just as I reached for the boy he confounded me, causing me to push instead. The boy hit his head hard against a rock and I saw blood. I also saw a good dent on the side of his head. If he *isn't* dead, he will be soon."

Crooked Nose grunted, looking around. "Where's the old man, then? I thought you had plans for all them, as well."

"Never mind him. He slipped away and I won't bother chasing." Lars explained. The crack of a whip sent the horses moving.

Briaca closed her eyes, squeezing back tears within her hood, quietly crying just as she used to over Mother. Only this time, she mourned Kado.

I'm sorry, Father, she prayed the gods would relay her message. *I wasn't strong enough to keep him safe!*

Chapter Three

Briaca felt her body being dragged first from the wagon and then through the mud. Her shoulder slammed against a doorframe as rough hands shoved her inside a building.

The meeting lodge? she wondered, assuming she would be put with the other young women. The hood was abruptly ripped free of her head.

Blinking, she looked around and took in her surroundings. Ten or so women stared back, all of whom she should recognize, but their faces were still a blur. Many had husbands off in the war, but several were in the same situation as she—waiting for the single men to return. Others, those whose children were taken, huddled together and mourned their loss.

Crooked Nose cut Briaca's bindings and shoved her hard to the floor. She rolled over, dazed and tired. Her ears had no choice but to listen to the distraught mothers.

"They'll be fine," one of them assured the others. "They're with the grandmothers."

"What do you think they'll do with them?" another asked.

"I'm sure we'll be reunited soon," the first insisted. "No one, not even Lars, would keep mothers separated from their children."

"Slaves," Briaca explained dryly. "I heard one say that Lars is gathering slaves. The fact Lord Eduard's men are aiding him suggests something happened to King Chilperic. I think Lars expects to be gifted these lands by Eduard."

"But why split us up?" the first mother demanded. "We'd go more willingly as families!"

"No," Briaca said, shaking her head. It throbbed from both fighting and dragging. "You won't see your children again. He'll sell or move us where we'll never see *anyone* we know. The youngest will grow up filled with lies and believing that slavery was better than death."

"Then why put them with the grandmothers?" the first mother demanded.

"Because he needs them to be taken care of until he doesn't any longer."

"Doesn't what?" the other asked.

"Doesn't need them," Briaca answered before closing her eyes. "He'll kill the elders or break their backs with hard labor."

"How can you say all this?" the first mother demanded.

"Because she isn't a mother," the other explained. "She's *stuck* taking care of that bratty brother of hers and doesn't understand true mother's love."

"Careful," warned Briaca. She had already tolerated as much from these women as she wanted. After the morning she had, arguing with Kado and then fighting against Lars' men, solitude sounded better than their company.

"She doesn't even know what mother's love is," the second added, "because hers hated children so much she left."

"I heard she left because their father beat her," a third tossed in.

"My father never beat any of us," Briaca said to the group, moving to a kneeling position and resting on her heels. "As for Mother, she loved us very much. Something must have happened to her."

"Oh, poor, poor girl," the first mother said. Briaca now clearly saw her face and recognized her as the baker's wife. No wonder she wasn't worried about serfdom. Bakers and artisans were rarely sold and neither were their families. "Is that the story your father told you?"

Briaca no longer cared what the others thought. Her hand lashed out and clapped the woman's ear. "I warned you that was enough about my mother. Don't blame *me* if you aren't ready to hear the truth about your children. You'll realize soon enough why they've been taken and understand quickly they won't be returned!"

The second mother was Clarisa, the wife of a sculptor. Both she and her husband had long ago adopted the Roman influence of their oppressors. She wore a flowing gown, flawless except for mud on its hem and her backside. "They won't have any choice but to return my son to *me*! My husband sculpted Lord Eduard's bust!"

Briaca let out a laugh, low and full of pity for these narrow minded women. "Fools," she said after they all had turned angry eyes toward her. "All of you are fools!"

They left her alone to her own thoughts after that, either pondering her warning or cursing her for saying it aloud. Either way they gave her silence. A few minutes later, the women inside all heard whips on the road as drivers drove away the carts.

Briaca's silence ended with a cacophony of mournful moans.

"Fools," she whispered, moving to a far corner away from their noise. Leaning against the wall she slumped and closed her eyes against the pain between her temples.

By nightfall, every woman in the longhouse hungered for more than the return of their children, with rumbling bellies and heads weak from exertion. Some had even collapsed with hopelessness, finally accepting Briaca's wisdom as truth. Soon after, horrible screams reached the women's ears followed by muffled wails. These came from the elder men of Cardac, those locked in the temple.

Briaca squeezed tears but held back the sobs that poured from the other women. Lars had stolen the useful from Cardac and killed what he deemed worthless. Only the women in this meeting lodge remained, but they too would be sorted and removed before long. Without care for her own fate, Briaca prayed for Kado and her father. After she had finished, she added one more for Mother.

At some point she fell asleep.

Chapter Four

In slumber Briaca found dreams and, among those, she found comfort. Standing at the entrance of a cave she watched as Argant the Storyteller waved his long walking staff, yellowed by age and more resembling ivory than wood. Carved along its length glowed ancient runes and text she could not read.

Kado lay wrapped in furs next to the fire, listening to a legendary tale of a dragon and its bonded vinculum, a man named Erwan. She had heard this story many times, only without the bloodsucking monsters the old man added in this telling. As he finished, the fire dimmed and the shadows deepened like Kado's breathing. The boy slumbered.

"Hello, Briaca," Argant said, old and feeble while leaning on his staff. She caught a better glimpse of the etched writing. It no longer glowed but still reflected the firelight. Resembling neither Roman nor Greek, she realized it was nothing like the Gaulish letters she knew, either.

"Hello, Argant," she replied, looking around. She knew she should be in the village, trapped in the meeting lodge with the other women, but did not wish to challenge this dream for fear of awakening. "You told him a different version of Erwan the Bold," she accused. "It was nothing at all like Mother's version."

"No, I told him the *true* version and will soon ensure he knows the rest of it as well."

Briaca let out a chuckle. "I never expected the word *true* would accompany *voltur* and *vampure*. I cringe with anticipation awaiting the rest."

The old man shrugged off her cynicism then turned, touching his staff to the rock wall behind him. A great portion of it swung away, opening inward and revealing a dark passage. After a shake, his staff glowed brightly as he stepped inside. "Come," he commanded, "you will awaken soon and we won't be able to talk further for some time."

She followed the bobbing light as it descended, curving around a wide turn. The moisture in the air grew thicker the deeper she stepped, musty and strangely foul. Cool air licked at her skin and stood up the hair on her arms. As she rounded the final bend she gasped. The tunnel had opened suddenly into another cavern, vast and more magnificent than the one above. The cool darkness wrapped them in silence.

I must return to Cardac, she urged herself, then scolded her own cowardice. *Kado needs me. So does father! So might even Mother, wherever she may be.* Trembling feet carried her forward.

The old man spoke. "They *all* need your vengeance! Only *you* are in a position to free the village from Lars!"

Briaca laughed. "I'm no fighter," she said.

"Yet you fought them when taken. I was there and saw your struggle."

"But I gave in and now am captive," she protested.

"No!" Argant's voice bellowed through the cavern. "Vengeance must guide you! Fuel it!"

"As I said, I am no fighter. I have taken care of Father's farm but, other than that, I am meant only to wed and bear children for my future husband."

"Lies!" accused Argant. "Inside you have ancient blood from a clan as old as time itself. Your brother understands this, as his yearning to bond a dragon proves." The light from his staff flashed, turning darkness into brilliance. Fires sprang up all around and Briaca flinched, trying to open her eyes against the painful light, but they refused.

The old man's staff is proof magic exists. It isn't wood, nor ivory... what is it? What has he carved upon to have such power?

Briaca shielded her eyes and, after opening them, realized Argant held his staff over the colossal remains of a dragon. Its yellowish tinge matched the skeleton exactly. All around, fires raged in the cavern, tall and searing they cast heat against her skin. "These tricks do not scare me, old man! You use light to disorient and confuse my senses. Besides, this is a dream and none of this is real."

The many fires flickered then surged brightly several times, casting strobing shadows around the chamber. Within their flashing, the skeleton seemed to move, stretching out its neck. It roared, blowing back Briaca's hair while sharp teeth snapped at her head. Its attack forced her to cower.

"Vengeance!" it roared angrily, its ancient breath snuffing out all the light in the room.

A soft glow slowly replaced the darkness and all was as it should have been. Argant smiled from beside the skeletal beast, his staff the only source of glow.

"But first you must go," the old man urged. "Fulfill your destiny and save your kindred bloodline." With the wave of his staff the skeletal dragon stood and shook dust from its bones. It fanned skinless wings which beat against the air with force, pushing it upward until disappearing into the shadows above.

As soon as the great beast was airborne, howling wind chilled the air, screeching and swirling inside the cavern. Soon the dragon hovered, snapping at invisible enemies on the wind.

"What does it fight?" Briaca asked the old man. "There's nothing there!"

"It fights an ancient evil, the same it fought so many eons ago. Why don't you see them, Briaca? Why do you say nothing is there?"

"Because there *isn't* anything there!" she protested.

"Only because the evil which surrounds you has not revealed itself. Rest assured it is there. It lurks in the nighttime, hides during the day, and craves your blood more than any other."

"Why mine?" she demanded. "I don't understand!"

Argant laughed again, the light of his staff snuffed, abruptly cutting the room to darkness. As the echo of his voice faded, Briaca realized he had slipped away and left her alone to ponder the meaning of it all.

All at once the dragon roared fire, casting shadows of winged beasts with human forms against the walls. These thrashed around as if alive, attacking the shadow of the dragon now locked in ghostly battle in the reflection. All at once they fell upon it, ripping off scales with sharp claws and biting the soft flesh waiting underneath. High above, the skeletal dragon fought nothing but air.

Briaca heard the scraping of footfalls on the floor behind her. She spun, expecting to find the old man had returned, but only met darkness. Once more the sound drew her attention, this time from both right and left. Again she turned this way then that but each time found nothing lurking.

The skeleton roared and breathed enough fire to nearly fill the cavern. This time, as Briaca turned to shield her eyes, she found the source of the scraping footsteps. Illuminated in a circle around her, she counted dozens of gaunt creatures perched on spindly legs, their skin greyed as if partially decomposed. Their stomachs bloated from malnourishment and their faces winced with pain as if the flames licked their bodies instead of the air. But what she noticed most were their teeth, long and needlelike with protruding fangs.

Voltur don't exist! she protested. This was only a dream. She said it louder, hoping the old man would hear. "Voltur don't exist!" All at once they rushed forward, clawing at her skin and pulling her onto the ground, each with the strength of five men. Fighting them off proved useless, as sharp teeth pierced her flesh. "None of this is real!"

From high above in the shadows a dragon answered with a roar.

Briaca awakened with a gasp, terrified by her dreams. They left her with a pounding chest and racing mind. But they were only dreams. Horrors like those in the cavern did not exist. The real monsters were men like Lars.

Across the meeting lodge the door slowly opened.

I can flee, wait till whoever enters comes in and run past them into the night, she reasoned. *It's dark and their eyes won't yet be adjusted.*

Carefully, she shifted her weight, quietly moving her body into position from which she could easily launch her escape. She watched as a dozen shadowy figures slithered inside, more resembling apparitions than men. Briaca readied herself, watching the door still ajar as the last figure entered.

Just as she raised, readying her hips to run, the slumbering women all around her slid past. Though no man had entered except those shadows, the other captives seemed to be dragged off without warning. They shot out of the room at incredible speeds, faster even then Briaca could run. Without further hesitation she made for the door.

Something grabbed her ankle and sent her crashing to the floor. She kicked. Strong and unrelenting it held on, refusing to let go. With eyes fixed on the open door she desperately fought, twisting her body to wrench free, and finally did. Scrambling, the girl raced toward freedom.

The door slammed shut.

From out of the shadows, Crooked Nose stepped out, his face gaunter than before. Shirtless, his bloated stomach bulged and his ribcage sunk inwards. As his lips curled into a smile, fangs descended from his mouth.

"Where are you going, girl?" he asked, cackling with laughter.

At first Briaca mistook this creature for a voltur, but he was unmistakably human. Besides, had he been one of those creatures he would never have walked in sunlight. A scraping announced whoever was behind her had come closer. She turned to find two voltur *had* escaped her dreams. These snarled hungrily, salivating over her blood.

"Get away from me," Briaca begged, but the creatures and Crooked Nose only moved closer.

They grabbed at her but she fought, hoping to overpower their smaller frames. Their strength surprised her, holding her tight while Crooked Nose moved in to feed.

Briaca ripped an arm free, cutting it against a razor sharp claw. As her fist crashed against the jaw of her attacker, a bit of her blood splattered across his face.

Enraged, Crooked Nose wiped it with his finger and sniffed. To Briaca's disgust he ran that finger across his tongue, tasting the tip as if it had been dipped in a sweet confection. His face immediately changed, less angry and seemingly amused. "Well now," he said. "It seems you're something much *different* than Lars expected." To the voltur he commanded, "Bind her but do not feast. Move her to the back room and lock her within."

The ghastly creatures led her away, kicking, fighting, and baring her teeth as if she were wilder and more dangerous than they.

Chapter Five

No one bothered Briaca until long after daybreak.

This room in which they locked her away was previously used for lodging, hosting visiting Roman dignitaries before the Gaulish uprising. The bed was unlike any she had ever slept upon and, despite her encounter with voltur, its feathered comfort had whisked her into dreamless sleep. That slumber did not last long, interrupted by anxious awakening.

Confusion filled her waking mind with more questions than she was prepared for answers. She stared at the ceiling and thought about Mother and Father, hearing the stories Oksana would tell her children.

Closing her eyes, she could imagine them all in that tiny cottage in the woods. Mother, as usual, told Kado's favorite tale of Erwan the Bold.

Her voice echoed in Briaca's mind, telling of the farmer who loved his family and how his children would run to meet him along the road each day as he left the fields for home. The story always made Briaca sad when she was younger, but she remained just as riveted as her brother. The worst part was when the children failed to arrive, and the farmer hurried up the road to find them all brutally slain by their Roman overseer, Dominus Titus.

It's just a story, she told herself, *to teach Gaulish children not to trust the Romans.* But she let her mind wander, remembering one night when a younger Briaca sat cross-legged at the feet of Oksana, and Kado rested in Mother's lap.

These were the best years, when their entire family was still together. All Briaca needed now was to see Father. That wait was not long and soon the door opened. A large man appeared, his yellow dark beard wild and full, giving him a bearish appearance. Only his eyes were gentle, a soft hazel just like Briaca's. She always thought she favored him more than Mother, and he never hid that he saw it too. He gave her a wink as he arrived.

Mother briefly paused her tale.

"Don't let *me* interrupt the story of Erwan the Bold!" he roared, giving his wife a kiss on the cheek before patting the head of each child. Briaca wrapped her arms around his leg and hugged it tightly.

She missed him so much and now wished he would return from war.

Mother continued, "He emerged from the forest, facing a rocky wall that seemed to reach the heavens. Erwan stared up at the peak high above, desperate to scale it in a single bound. But night impeded his travels, him having spent all day burying his wife and children."

"And so he rested," Father added from across the room, "as all good fathers should after a long day." He gestured to his boots and Kado hopped from Mother's lap, racing to do his nightly task. Turning away from father he straddled the boot, gripping the heel of it with his hands. Father gently placed the other boot against his son's buttocks and pushed, sending the boy toppling to the floor amid gleeful laughs. Briaca rushed to remove the other in the same way. "Go on, dear," Conrad urged his wife, "please continue."

"And so he rested," she agreed. "He camped all night on the edge of the forest, and awoke at first light. Heartbroken, he found the mountain had not changed. There was no scaling the slippery rocks, and no other way up or around the barrier."

"But he found a way!" little Kado exclaimed, climbing once more onto his mother's lap.

"Yes, there is always a way around a problem if you know where and when to look," she agreed. "As the sun rose higher he stared upward, building the courage to climb. Just as he was about to attempt what would surely result in death, he found the path. Upward he walked all morning and afternoon, very careful not to look down. He did so only once, and the vertigo of that single misstep nearly cost his life, but he eventually reached the summit."

"And then he found dragons!" Father roared, standing and raising his arms like a monster. Kado and Briaca laughed and scrambled to get away as he chased them both to bed. Catching each one with a giant hug he devoured them with kisses before tucking them in.

"Finish the story, Mother!" Kado begged from the safety of his blankets.

"Tomorrow I will. Everything is better when fully revealed by first light," she said with a smile.

"But nothing was ever fine," Briaca said into the empty room, shaking free of the memory. "That's the night she left us." This was also the night Kado grew so fascinated by dragons he would never shut up about them.

The next morning, after discovering Oksana had left without even a note, he swore to his father and sister to someday climb Mount Sapientia and bond an aerouant. Then he would fly around the entire Roman Empire in search of Mother.

Briaca knew better. There were no such things as dragons, only bad things and demons in the night—evil that lurked and lured out mother then started wars that dragged Father away. That same unfairness had stolen her adolescent years and forced her into responsibilities before she was ready.

Remembering the nightmare in the lodge, she added voltur to that list of evil. *They were real,* she admitted to herself. The recent memory of shadowy creatures dragging away the other women sent shivers down her spine.

A key rattled a lock and the door to her room was pushed open.

Briaca sat up, moving as close to the wall and as far away from the newcomer as possible. She recognized him immediately, with his ruggedly handsome face, muscled body, and long red hair. His eyes swam like pools of darkness, red and no longer green. He wantonly looked her up and down as if tasting her skin. This made her cringe further away.

Lars ignored her disgust and sat on the edge of the bed. "You were supposed to go to Aventicum and be sold with the other women," he explained, "but I am told you are special."

"I'm nothing of the sort," she answered with defiance. "I'm a nobody, not worth anything to anyone. You should let me go."

"No, I think I'll keep you around until I figure out *what* you are."

"I saw voltur, last night. Who are *you* to have such monsters in your employ?"

"What are *you* that they want so badly to consume your sanguis?"

"You keep saying *what*. Don't you mean *who*?"

"You will learn very soon, girl, that I always say exactly what I mean. *What* are you?"

"Like I said, I'm nobody."

Without warning Lars grabbed her wrist and pulled it toward a knife he suddenly held in his right hand. He moved with lightning quickness, faster than Briaca had ever seen another human. Before she even knew he held her wrist, her palm bled a crimson line. The warlord scooped this onto his blade and spread it across his tongue, tasting her flavor as a chef would judge stew.

"Interesting," he finally said after smacking his lips and briefly closing his eyes. When he opened them, the red had darkened and each swam like pools of blood. Neither had whites nor pupils. These examined her body as if lusting after more of what she had to offer.

That look repulsed Briaca. She wrenched away her hand and scurried further into the corner.

"So it's true," he whispered, shaking free of his trance. His eyes blinked to green, normal and human, and he softly smiled as if nothing had happened. "You are special indeed."

"What was the purpose of that? Will you feed me to your voltur?"

Lars shrugged. "That depends."

"Depends on what?" she demanded.

"On what you know and what you can offer me."

"You'll get nothing because I *know* nothing!"

The warlord abruptly stood, crossing to the far side of the room. Briaca took that moment to try and flee, rushing to the door but finding it securely locked. Lars made no move to stop her. He merely settled into a chair against the far wall and slumped backward, crossing his legs and resting both hands atop his belly. He closed his eyes as if still savoring the taste of her blood.

"Tell me a story, then," he finally said. "Surely you know the one about Erwan the Bold. Isn't that a favorite around Gaul?"

"Wouldn't *you* know? You're not Roman."

"Alas, I'm also not a Gaul. I come from farther north than the Romans ever conquered. But that's not important. Tell me the story. I'm certain you know it."

Briaca gave up trying to turn the knob and slumped back onto the bed. "I *hate* that story," she complained, hoping to be spared.

"Such a shame," he *tsked*. "I wanted so badly to hear your version. Why don't you allow *me* to tell a story? I want so badly to share the *real* version."

"Do I have any choice?" she demanded.

"Not really."

"Then it seems you have a *captive* audience."

"Witty!" Lars exclaimed with excitement and a broad grin. The tips of his canine teeth seemed sharper than before. "I love wit," he explained, "and especially sarcasm. Only the intelligent understand it."

"I don't care," Briaca snapped.

"No? Would you rather hear my story?" Lars asked, his words dripping with sarcasm. Briaca shot him an angry look that meant she understood his joke. "See? You're clearly not a *nobody,* you're smarter than the average human."

She said nothing in reply, no longer wishing to encourage his banter. To her chagrin he began telling his version of the story.

"Many centuries ago, after the Romans first conquered Gaul, they chose overseers to stay behind and collect tribute for the empire.

That rank was called *Dominus* and Titus was among those who wore that badge upon his robes. He presided over the Aventicum seat but served a different master, above even the Emperor to whom he publicly swore."

"A man cannot serve two masters," Briaca pointed out. "My father taught me that."

"And where is your father now?"

"You know very well he serves King Chilperic as a pikeman."

"Yes, and Lord Eduard as well, and will no doubt die honorably upon the battlefield just as Chilperic has."

Briaca could not believe her ears. The audacity of this man to suggest... Then she understood his meaning, why the king's men had been in Cardac. "King Chilperic is dead?"

"Not yet, but mortally wounded and expected to die very soon. Lord Eduard leads the final push against the Romans, and his victory has been ordained by our mutual master."

"I don't understand."

Lars smiled broadly. His teeth had returned to normal. "Of course you don't. You also don't listen very well. I just told you that Dominus Titus privately served two masters. So do Lord Eduard and I, and so does Alan."

She frowned.

"Alan is my right-hand man whom you punched in the jaw last night."

"Crooked Nose..." she realized, reliving the memory of the voltur. She shivered.

"No longer an accurate description, I assure you, but yes. That was Alan. Like Dominus Titus once served the Romans. Alan serves me, I serve Lord Eduard, and we all served King Chilperic. But even he served a master, just as the Roman Emperor does as well, even if they did not realize who wields the real power and pulls the marionette strings from behind the veil."

"So you're saying your other master pulls those strings?"

"Precisely."

"And I guess you're one of those strings moving others. Do you get pulled along with those your master tugs?"

Lars grinned even wider. "See? I knew you were bright. You pieced together what even King Chilperic could not."

"Is that why he's dead?"

Lars shrugged. "I don't know *every* string that's pulled, but I can guess. Lord Eduard will be elevated by those who also serve our master and will do so because it fits his plan."

"That's why you're here, why you sold away the women and carted off their children and grandmothers? What will be done with the elder men? What will Father and the other soldiers find in Cardac when they return?"

"The elder men no longer need *anything* done. Last night they were consumed in a grand feast."

Briaca felt the world around her spin. Her heart skipped a beat and thumped hard in her chest, realizing all those screams were those men being eaten alive. "You're cannibals?" she asked disbelieving.

"No, not at all. Nothing of the sort." Lars flashed a wide smile that once more revealed his canine teeth had changed, now fully descended and sharp as needles at the tips. "We would *never* consume our own species. To do so would bring certain death. So we feast on humans instead, but only their blood and not their flesh, and, when we can find them, we feast upon the sanguis of dragons."

Astonished by his admission, Briaca almost missed that he had mentioned dragons. "Dominus Titus was the evil overseer who murdered the family of Erwan the Bold, at least in the version my mother told. Erwan had come home to find the Roman had taken his wife and killed his beloved children, that's why he sought a dragon to bond. He sought vengeance against the evil man."

"That *is* the version humans like to tell, but I assure you it is another lie spread by dragons. They even tell a *different* version, like that you heard last night."

This entire conversation felt strange to Briaca. It all came so fast and was difficult to believe. She eyed him keenly, guessing at his game. "You're a peddler of lies veiled in truth, aren't you? You're telling me all this, rambling arrogantly along because you want to impress, intending to either kill or persuade me into your fold. Well, kill me dead because I'm not interested."

Lars shrugged. "Not all death is permanent. You learned *that* last night."

He means the voltur. Her skin crawled at the memory. Voltur were not only real, they took on human form as well. *He hasn't tried to make me one,* she realized. *He's putting it off for some reason.*

She pointed at her palm and the crimson line now slowly scabbing over. "When you tasted my blood, you did not drink it directly with your lips. Why?"

"How observant," Lars replied, running his tongue up and down his fangs. "I did not wish to taint you in case Alan was wrong about your origin. Once a vampure feasts upon dragon sanguis they transform and are never the same. You are not a dragon, but I can taste a bit of their bloodline lurking in your sanguis. To have you now, in my custody, ensures my next form awaits. I will become an *equal* to Lord Eduard, just for claiming you as nourishment."

Dragons. Transform. This man was not only mad, his mind had descended into full derangement. *He'll kill me,* she realized, *by drinking my blood like he did the old men.* She tried to stall. "But we digress. You haven't yet told me the story of Dominus Titus, or the real version of Erwan the Bold."

Lars could no longer hide his hunger, his hands trembling and his mouth drooling to quench a lustful thirst. "What is your name, girl?"

"Briaca."

"You're very intelligent, Briaca, but you don't know everything. Vampure do not waste time telling stories around campfires. We're not dragons. We inject our heritage directly into those we consume." In the blink of an eye the warlord had crossed the full length of the room, his fangs extended and snapping as he ran. Before she could flinch, his fangs bit deep into her neck.

Chapter Six

Briaca barely felt the bite.

The crisp snapping of tissue almost seemed far away as if she had merely pricked a finger against a thorn, only without pain. What filled her was disgust, causing the girl to nearly retch as his mouth touched her skin. This man whom she hated so much, who represented everything wrong with her world, violated her person with the closeness of hot breath and wet saliva, slurping and sucking at the wound. The tender caress of his tongue lapped up the drippings, causing her to scream.

That scream died in an instant, her repulsion replaced by euphoria. Her eyes grew wide with want, accepting this violation instead of fighting him off. Lars magically controlled her somehow, had entered her mind and made it his. He willed Briaca to obey his every command as he gently laid her body against the soft feather mattress.

"No," she protested in a whisper, but that word only pushed his mouth more firmly against her neck. Thankfully, he seemed content to drink his fill and not to violate her further.

Father had warned him what a man could do to a woman, and that was why he had given her that knife when he left. *Men will listen to steel,* he had told her at the time, *when they will not heed reason.*

Do I still have the blade? she wondered. *Have they taken it from me?* She reached underneath her skirt, feeling the soft skin of her own inner thigh. She found the knife still strapped where no righteous man would search. It was a dagger, thin enough to remain hidden and long enough to do harm. With a single, practiced motion, she drew the blade and moved to plunge it between his ribs.

It shattered into pieces that fell onto the mattress.

Lars pulled his mouth from her neck and explained. "I am not human. I am descended from a bloodline as ancient as yours and cannot be harmed by steel." He slurped and then licked a trail of blood as it ran down her neck. Pulling away he moved again to the empty chair and slumped exhausted. "I feel your blood as it works inside of me. I want to drink so much, to drain you dry, but I am not as cruel as you believe. You and the other villagers see me as an opportunist, a warlord who flexes muscle to exact tribute for Lord Eduard. Don't you see I'm not the villain? I am merely the messenger."

"Then why did you steal the women and children?" she asked drowsily, rolling over to better see her captor. His eyes swirled and his face had contorted. Where his skull had once appeared human, the bones had shifted and ridges appeared on his cheeks and brow. He now seemed a human version of the voltur—only more noble instead of wretched.

"I followed the orders of my master. The death of King Chilperic has ushered in a new system of landownership, one that will some-day spread across all of Europe and most of Asia. Once he is king, Eduard will reward his vassals with parcels of land and the people will be redistributed to live upon it. They will *convey* with it even while those noble families come and go."

"No human should be slave to another," Briaca slurred, slipping into a dream world.

"I agree and so does Goro. That's why, under feudalism, they will be slaves to the *land* and the nobles will provide for both. You will someday see, just as the world will, this new system will bring prosperity and longer life to all. Our master *cares* for his humans, just as *they* in turn care for their livestock."

Briaca had to fight to keep her eyes open. The sensation dragged her down as the man in the chair blurred before her eyes. "*Our* master?" she demanded. "I do not serve *your* master."

"Only because you have not yet met him," Lars insisted. "Close your eyes and you will understand. Give in to sleep and Goro will make his own introduction."

Unable to fight it, the sensation won out. As the room and Lars disappeared, Briaca descended into darkness. Soon she plummeted from the sky. The bed, the room, even Lars had disappeared.

Wind rushed by as she fell, stinging her eyes as she tried to look around. The ground rose closer as if to punish her leaving. She rolled, afraid to face her death, and looked upward toward the clouds as a voice echoed in her mind.

They fell in great numbers from the heavens, those cast down by the Creator.

The impact of her landing shook the earth, sending rocks scattering high into the air. Dust and debris flew even higher. All across the hemisphere dozens of craters and plumes announced Briaca had not fallen alone.

Who? she asked the voice. *Who fell?*

All around the world androgynous people stood from the craters, unharmed and not soiled by their descension. They emerged beautiful, alluring, and smiling over their newfound domains.

The voice continued speaking. *Each of the Keryx ruled their own dominion, disinterested in each other, happy to have shed their god and live as one themselves. These Titans discovered mankind, herded them into villages like penned livestock. They chose wives from among these humans, spreading their seed and extending their bloodlines.*

Briaca watched with horror as these beings, once brilliant and shining, twisted into evil creatures without feeling or remorse. Uncaring that these humans rejected their love, the Keryx relentlessly forced themselves and laughed at the screams for mercy. Who would bring such mercy? The gods of these people were different than he who cast them down, they walked upon Earth.

These women bore children to the Keryx, powerful Nephilim more glorious than their fathers who rose as giants. Each avenged their mother by toppling their sire, devouring his soul and assuming his former glory.

But these children were not human, not as Briaca expected. Though some walked on two legs and resembled their mothers, some took on the form of creatures. She counted twelve in all, each lining up for her inspection.

Early man knew their names and some still linger in myth and legend. What is forgotten is the war they fought after three betrayed their cousins.

A massive sea beast, a broad-winged raptor, and a fiery creature cast in molten rock joined forces against their siblings. Soon a shadowy specter joined the three, making their number four.

Toppled by deceit, Peace, Virtue, and Righteousness lay defeated at their feet. Briaca looked down and mourned along with Fire, Illusion, and Beast. Unlike the humanoids on the ground, these Titans more closely resembled monsters. Only two Nephilim remained upon two feet, striking images of their beautiful fathers. Blood bowed his head in reverence then urged his siblings to rally. Might, strong and powerful and wielding a magical blade imbued with light, echoed with a roaring call to battle.

Might led us against our betrayers and a terrible battle ensued as the remaining five fought against four. War raged without regard for the humans of the land, forcing them into caves to escape devastation. I lamented but Fire did not. He called their losses collateral, as pawns upon the board who shielded our flanks as we made progress in the war.

Fire, it turned out, resembled a massive dragon fighting on land and in the sky. He met the condor in the air for which it was named, catching his brother with massive jowls and pounding him lifeless against the ground.

I urged Fire to join myself and Might as we squared off against Sea and Earth. But deception lurked in his eyes. I feared he had been lost.

Illusion and Beast stood back, hesitantly watching the fray, but they did not cower. They waited instead for opportunity. When his attention was turned by Illusion, Beast leapt upon Shadow with sharp claws. These two fought, bit, and scratched at one another, until Illusion cut the air around them like a knife along a curtain.

A shimmering portal opened and the trio slipped through to another realm, lost to us and whereabouts unknown. Might tried to save our cousins, sheathing his blade and reaching in to grab them, but held up empty hands as the rip between realms sealed. He drew his blade and cut a new slice between space and time, then leapt in to follow, find, and retrieve our allies.

That left only Fire and Blood against Earth and Sea. The massive beast of molten rock swung wildly at both, but Blood leapt into the sky, his broad, leathery wings avoiding what would have been a killing blow. Fire took the full brunt of it but did not fall. Instead he roared with laughter and began ripping apart his cousin and thrashing about in the searing heat. He acted as if he splashed in a cool puddle of rain instead of the fiery demise of a Titan.

I moved to attack Sea, racing toward him with as much speed as I could fly. Without Might and the others, I worried how I would defeat him. I was humanoid and he was the colossus of the deep, the ever shifting creature of the watery dominion. He transformed to a great kraken, lashing forth with tentacles that forced me to fly higher out of his reach. But I kept his attention long enough for Fire to finish off this cousin as well.

The massive dragon raced toward the kraken. His teeth, now singed black from devouring Earth, ripped into soft flesh and drove the beast into the ocean depths. Blood hovered above, watching as the pair disappeared beneath stormy waves.

I waited, watching for any sign Fire had triumphed, but when he finally emerged, he did so, filled with rage, angry to have merely driven the traitor into the abyss. He turned those angry eyes toward me, fiery and filled with hatred as if I too had betrayed him. We fought in the sky and on dry land, but neither of us dared to journey once more into the briny sea.

Vampure and dragon squared off silently, staring at each other with hatred and anger in their swirling eyes of blood and fire. A stalemate, they agreed to divide their dominion into two parts.

The descendants of dragonkind would rule the mountains and the lands to the west, while I settled with the fertile valleys and farmlands to the east. Of course, the continents shifted over time and those mountains grew taller, but we avoided each other as long as we could. Fire found a way to further his bloodline without involving humans, lording over them as their master, and dragons grew numerous.

Briaca watched as thousands of dragons dotted the land and filled the skies above. They became numerous, but not nearly so as the human slaves they carefully cultivated to raise the beasts and crops both needed for survival.

I was not so lucky. Our kind could only reproduce with our saliva, and I set out to hand select my descendants, judging the worthiest among humans. Fire never allowed us to live in peace, and his descendants attacked us often and without mercy. He drove us underground into caves and catacombs, but eventually I found a way for my children to walk among the humans. We hid among them.

The world faded from Briaca's mind and darkness replaced the images. Blinking, she opened her eyes to find Lars still resting in the chair beside her bed.

"You are a descendent of Blood?" she asked more coherently than before, her thoughts nearly once more her own.

"Goro," Lars nodded agreement, "is what he goes by now. The great war never ended between Fire and Blood, and you are proof the Ancient One found a way to involve humans into his bloodline."

"I don't understand," Briaca admitted. Lars no longer loomed with as much evil presence as before. He appeared compassionate, almost contrite for involving her, but most off all seemed exhausted by the consumption of her blood. "Please explain why you say I share the bloodline of dragons," she begged.

"I will in time," Lars promised. "But first we both need rest. I have consumed much of your sanguis and you must recover and restore what I took."

"Sanguis…" Briaca had heard that word so many times on this day. "That is the Roman word for blood."

"Yes, but they oversimplify the word they learned from our kind. Sanguis is the lifeforce of every creature. It contains the living soul and resides there in the blood just as ichor stores the power of the Nephilim. Since we are descended from Titans, our sanguis is mixed with the human blood of our ancestors and imbues our minds with their memories, like those you just witnessed, and also holds the power each entity passed on."

Briaca's mind swam with a desire to sleep and closed her eyes. "So the others? The other Keryx? They passed on their ichor into humans the same way?"

"That is a question for Goro, but I believe so, yes. Those who reproduced passed their ichor into sanguis. Briaca, please know I did not wish you harm, only to enlighten you to the truth about the world. That ancient battle still rages, and you are now a part of it."

"I don't want to be," Briaca protested. Sleep was overtaking her mind, and she yawned and leaned back on the mattress. "It doesn't concern me at all."

"Goro has empowered our kind with an ability to recognize those most worthy to join our ranks. The rest we devour or feed to the lowly voltur. I know you are worthy and, no matter what you once were, you are now one of us."

"I don't want to be," a drowsy Briaca muttered. "I hate you," she whispered before falling asleep.

Chapter Seven

Briaca stared into the glass. Though she had never seen a mirror, she knew what they were. But this one had fanciful carvings and a rich silver frame. It screamed wealth with its audacity. It reflected a man, a Roman by his attire, staring back with worried eyes. She knew her own face and wondered how she saw this man instead. His wavy hair seemed untamable despite the ivory comb in his hand. Something bothered him deeply, and he seemed to put off whatever it was he should be doing.

From down the hall a deep voice called, "Titus! Where is my son?"

"You need to answer him," a woman suggested, rolling over in a large bed and poking her face out from beneath the covers. She was older, at least older than the face in the mirror, and seemed amused at Briaca's silence. "He'll have you flogged if you make him late. It's *your* day, after all."

Briaca realized the woman talked to her, or rather to this young man, but said nothing, afraid she would speak in her own voice. To her surprise the young man spoke instead.

"This is *hardly* my day, Diana. It seems more of another befitting Father. He's demanded this of me since the day I was born."

"Titus!" the voice called again.

"He is in here, Dominus," Diana replied. Briaca turned and found her sitting on the edge of the bed, completely nude and already sipping wine despite the early hour.

A large man, dressed in the robes of a Roman aristocrat, barged into the room, ignoring the woman. "It's time to go!" he warned his son. "This day only comes *once* for a Roman!"

Briaca glanced once more at the young man in the reflection, he seemed so scared, then followed.

The building turned out a palace. Though she gushed at the beauty, the young man still lacked amusement for the day. He followed his father dutifully, but his tone reeked with irritability.

"I don't want to go to Gaul, Father," Briaca heard the young man say with her mouth. To her surprise the aristocrat only laughed.

"No Roman *wants* to go to Gaul!" he explained. "But we have business there, and you were selected for this title ten years before I earned mine. Don't you see? If you do well here, you will be made a Senator like you desire!"

Briaca felt her shoulders shrug. Apparently titles meant nothing to this young man.

As the pair approached a large door guarded by two soldiers, his father held up his hand to delay them from announcing his arrival. "Titus," he explained, "our duty is not only to Emperor Augustus Octavian. You are about to meet *him*."

"Meet who, Father?"

"You will learn that very soon. Just know that there is no saying *no* to this man. He's not even a man, if truth be told. He's one of the gods."

Briaca shuddered as chills ran down her spine. As the dominus nodded to the soldiers, the door opened into a private room. She followed the nobleman inside, feeling Titus jump as the doors slammed shut behind him. He covered his nerves by kneeling before the emperor.

"Hail Caesar," Titus proclaimed, "Herald of Pax Augusta, Heir to Julius, and divine Auctoritas of Cultus Imperius."

Briaca noticed Titus' father failed to demonstrate the same courtesies. Even the emperor himself looked away without even the briefest of ceremony. Both men turned their attention to another in the room. To him the dominus knelt in prostrate, kissing the easterner's sandals.

"You did not prepare him?" the easterner asked, dressed in fine clothing. Briaca found him young and beautiful, even if he was short.

His accent reminded her of some Judaean migrants she had briefly met stopping in Cardac on their way to Aventicum. His question seemed to accuse the dominus.

"I tried, Great Lord, but we have not had a moment for privacy since we left Rome."

"He is confused," the easterner remarked. "Explain it to him, Octavian."

The emperor cleared his throat and spoke with the eloquence of a trained orator, practiced and proven on the senate floor itself. "I first travelled to this land of Gaul in the Roman year 27. It was widely reported I had fallen ill at that time. What was not told to the empire was why I had travelled here in the first place. I owed tribute to this man, Goro of Ripa Pannonica, for helping me win the war against Marc Antony. I would not be emperor today if not for his aid."

Titus looked at his father, now standing as he bowed his head before Goro. "You called this man *Lord*, and said in the hall he is a god. You said we owe him our duty. I see no god, Father, only a man."

The face of the dominus paled with shock at his son's blatant disrespect. Even Emperor Augustus appeared worried, but Goro only laughed.

"Spoken like a true Roman!" he said. "You are observant and wise, young Titus. Your father seems to have prepared you for the role after all." He turned to the emperor and held out his hand. "Grovel before me, Octavian. Kiss my hand and speak once more your vow."

Briaca watched, sharing the shock of Titus, as Caesar Augustus slid off his throne and lay flat on the floor at Goro's feet.

"I am not worthy to kiss your hand, Lord Goro, my master and true Cultus Imperius. My life is not my own. I owe my existence solely to you and beg your forgiveness for any transgressions I may utter while acting on your behalf. My blood is of your blood, my mind is of your mind, and my actions are ordained by your hand. I am your weapon, your tool, and an extension of your grace."

Goro ignored the emperor's oath, stepped over his prostrated body, and walked closer to Titus, eyeing him closely as if looking into his soul. Briaca feared he could see through the illusion and view her instead of the young man. "Leave us," he said to Augustus and Dominus Flavus. "I want to speak to this young man alone."

Both men jumped to their feet and scurried from the room.

"Hmm," he said appraisingly. "You are both shocked and intrigued by what you've seen. I guess you've never seen Flavus make a fool of himself to anyone but Octavian?"

"No sir," Titus admitted. "It is odd to witness your power, but I always assumed someone else pulled their strings, so I am not completely surprised. Father is weak, a sycophant to any with power, and has no compass to guide him except ambition."

"But you are not ambitious? I thought they brought you here today to make you *Dominus* Titus over Aventicum."

Titus nodded. "That is what I was told as well, but it is not a position I wanted."

"Surely there is *some* ambition in you."

"I want to orate in the senate, to ensure prosperity for all citizens of the empire."

"I see. You have ambition but not for yourself. You wish to use your position to aid others?"

"Yes... Goro." Titus made a concerted effort not to call this man *sir* or *lord* when he spoke.

"What if I told you that I can give you that power, to balance out not just the empire but the world?"

"Power is a mistress. As soon as a man grows comfortable with her in his arms, she leaves him for another just as quickly as she arrived."

Goro laughed again but abruptly stopped, his eyes narrowing as he grabbed both Titus's shoulders. "I am no man, and thus power obeys my *every* command." His blue eyes suddenly turned red. Even the whites and his black pupils turned crimson, swirling like pools of blood. Briaca found them oddly hypnotic.

His face and body changed. High ridges rose up on his cheeks and brow, just as Briaca had witnessed on Lars. But a circle of horns emerged from this man, forming a crown around Goro's head. In front of her eyes he grew, as the bones in his body shifted, swelled, and elongated. As his shoulders widened, a thick hump formed between the blades. Then two wings emerged, long and leathery while reaching more than twice as wide as he was tall.

Goro's voice echoed in her head and she recognized him as the narrator from the earlier telling of the Keryx.

I took Titus as one of my most favorites, specially chosen among my highest lords. Because he was an honest man, I loved him more than Caesar Augustus. I wept when he died at the hands of our enemies and swore vengeance against their bloodline when I raised him.

Why are you showing me him? Briaca demanded. *I know the story of Erwan the Bold, and I know this man was no seeker of balance. He was a rapist and a murderer, not a benevolent leader.*

You believe the lies of dragonkind, Goro insisted. *They have poisoned your mind with tales of their moral superiority. Dragons view mankind as their subjects, like cattle to cull without reason.*

Did Titus not kill *Erwan's family?* she demanded. *Was that part of the legend also constructed from lies?*

Soon I will reveal to you the full story of Dominus Titus and the truth about his war with Erwan the Insignificant!

Briaca froze in place as Goro leaned in with long fangs and bit into the neck she shared with Dominus Titus. As he pulled away with blood trickling down his chin, she realized this creature was the same vampure who fought against the dragon in her earlier vision. Goro was the Keryx, the Lord of Blood she had witnessed do battle for eons against his sworn enemy the Lord of Fire.

Chapter Eight

"Fight them," a voice urged, booming in Briaca's mind. It was Argant the Storyteller. "Fight Goro and resist him with all your strength! Help is coming!"

"I can't," she protested. "I'm already bit."

"It's not too late. You are special and I know a way!"

Why me? she wondered. "I'm *not* special!"

"Yes, you are." Argant briefly materialized in front of the girl, standing radiantly against a dark background. "Lars was right about one thing—you are very special indeed but even more so now. Goro has chosen you as one of his high lords!"

As quickly as he arrived Argant had gone, replaced by a Roman soldier charging her line.

"Pikemen!" a voice cried out from behind. "Hold!"   Briaca and the men on both sides tried but the soldier's impact caused one pikeman to lose his footing. It was done, the line had broken.

"Regroup!" the commander yelled as reserves rushed to fight as more Romans rushed by. They charged a squad of knights who formed a ring around their king.

King Chilperic. Briaca recognized the man as he swung his blade from horseback. Before his reserves could reach him, his saddle was cut by a Roman legionary. As the horse fell out from under the sovereign, he was dragged to the ground. All at once the enemy was upon him, pounding his armored body with their blades.

"Conrad!" one of the pikeman screamed, jabbing Briaca in the ribs to get her attention. "Reform!" the man next to her begged.

Conrad? she marveled. *Father?* Then she understood. What she viewed was through his eyes. King Chilperic had fallen and would indeed be gravely wounded if not killed. She fell into line with the others and braced her body against the line.

Turning her head once more, Briaca watched as Lord Eduard rode upon the bloodbath. Leaping from his own mount he landed solidly on his feet and snarled at the Romans. She blinked as long fangs descended from his gums. In a flurry he cut down soldiers with awesome might, stronger than ten men it seemed. His eyes swam red with blood.

Even Eduard is one of them, she marveled. Suddenly she was no longer battling the Romans and was instead enveloped by blackness.

Briaca, a woman's voice echoed in Briaca's mind. *Why don't you remember the words of the story as I taught you?*

Mother? she asked the phantom. *Which story? Where are you? Why did you leave us?*

Ignoring her questions, Mother asked again, *Do you not remember the words?*

Oksana's voice lured Briaca to a place from her childhood. Kado sat upon his mother's lap. Briaca sat cross-legged in her usual spot in front of the hearth. Her eyes were large with interest, listening intently to the story their mother told. She briefly broke them away to meet her brother's, giving him a wink and smile.

I've already seen this! Briaca cried out in her mind. *Do not show it to me again!*

"And then he found dragons!" Father roared, standing and raising his arms like a monster.

The room and her family fell away once more into darkness, and Briaca abruptly stood before a tomb hidden under dense foliage. Her brother was there, standing with a small dragon.

"*Thoir an aire do na h-uile a ta ciontachadh,*" the creature read aloud. "Beware all who trespass."

"Did the voltur leave that as a warning?" Kado asked.

"I think not." The dragon's fiery eyes swirled with mystery while considering the possibilities. "I did not expect to find something such as this, not here."

"Why not?"

"This predates the people of this land, back to a time of the Ancient Ones."

"Ancient Ones…" Kado considered her words. "You called Argant that, and so did the elder dragons."

The dragon, an aerouant by its long, snakelike body, puffed out a held breath clearing dust and debris from the base of the worn obelisk. She focused on a freshly revealed line of runic text.

"*Fon talamh tha deamhain*," she read. "Demons lie within."

The world around Briaca abruptly spun out of control. The inky blackness changed, shimmering and growing noticeably warmer. Her mind wavered, unable to bear the skin searing heat. She paused, standing still and peering into the blackness. One by one, ghostly fires appeared, illuminating row after row of army tents. Father sat before one, quietly sipping tea from a tin mug.

"My son and daughter," Conrad told his companion, a man dressed in the same pikeman's cote, "are all alone. That's who I'll return to after the war."

"No missus?" the other soldier asked.

"She went away." His father replied in the same manner he had always answered Kado and Briaca, without emotion and not wishing to elaborate.

"What does that even mean?" the soldier laughed, earning hushing sounds from the other fires. Quieter he asked, "Why would your wife just leave?"

"She had… She had something… some pressing obligation to take care of, a task she once said was more important than anything else she could do as a wife or mother."

"And you let her go?"

The voice of Goro once more intruded upon Briaca's mind, speaking as gently as a father would scold a child.

Ignore the lies of the Ancient One! He is teller of falsehoods, a storyteller of fables intended to deceive you! Resist him! Resist and

I will show you the truth of your family! Have you never wondered why your mother left?

Once more her vision swam, then settled on the warm firelight inside her father's cabin. This time she blended with her mother just as she had done once before with Titus.

Oksana stole a glance at her sleeping children then returned to knitting. Kado had fallen asleep first, his day so full of activity he could not handle any more. Briaca had resisted, her stubbornness so much like her fathers, but eventually drifted off.

"They're getting too big for me to chase around and wrestle," Conrad said from his chair. Though his eyes were closed her husband would try not to sleep until his wife had followed him to bed. "I think I pulled something in my back," he added with a smile. He loved his children dearly, as much as he loved Oksana.

"You came home late," she pointed out, finally addressing the irritation she had hidden from the children. "What grim news do you bring?" she demanded.

"One of Lord Eduard's men called us away from our labor. A king's man addressed all of us in Cardac."

Oksana stiffened. Grim news indeed, for a king's man to call a meeting of the men. "And? Who are we warring against now?" she demanded.

"He was vague, saying we were threatened by a *Roman threat,* but said nothing more."

"The real threat is here, in the kingdom, and it wears the king's clothing!" she snapped, her disdain for their sovereign's lineage unbridled. He was not a Gaul like her husband, the king's line spurred from the Romans, a patsy to their empire. "We grow poorer" she complained, "while he fattens from *our* labor!"

"I think that explains the threat," Conrad said, echoing the thoughts of other men in the town. "Some of us believe there's finally been a revolt, he's risen against the Romans and joined the Franks north of Aventicum."

"And he'll waste every one of *you* until the empire quells it!" she added scornfully. "This *isn't* your fight!"

"No, but I won't be able to refuse once they stop taking volunteers. Soon they'll impress those who hold back. At least by joining up now I'll be trained in a specialty."

"A specialty?" she demanded. "Like waiving a pike around on the front lines?"

Conrad flinched but did not answer.

Oksana regretted her words at once. He was a brave man, but fear lurked beneath his calmness. He needed to believe he could survive better with a pike in his hands than with a pitchfork. *When King Chilperic is finished, all weapons will lay discarded upon the battlefield*, she mused. "I'm sorry," she told him. "Why don't you wash up and go to bed. I've some things to finish before I can join you."

Conrad stood, bending to kiss the top of her head before moving his boots from the hearth. "Don't stay up late," he begged his wife. "I won't be able to sleep until you're beside me."

"I know," she said through a feigned smile, "and I won't. I promise I'll be right behind you." Oksana waited until the bedroom door shut before throwing down her knitting. Only then did the tears fall, a blend of sorrow and anger toward the king.

A soft rap at the door dried them as quickly as they had started. There was no telling who had business at this hour. Jumping to her feet she eyed the bedroom door. Conrad should answer, but he needed rest more than she.

With discernment enough to look out the peephole, she spied Argant the Storyteller standing in the moonlight outside.

Without hesitation Oksana opened the door and stepped out to join him.

"It's begun," he told her.

"Just as you foretold," she agreed.

"Just as you once made a pledge to give aid," he reminded the woman.

"I was a child then, no older than Kado."

"It's the only way," the old man said without looking away. His eyes drilled into hers, searching for a single waver in her resolve.

"But if he goes away to fight, the children will need me!"

"*When* he goes away to fight, you and the children will answer to your own fates and he will return home to empty beds and a lonely hearth. Only *you* can do this!"

Oksana turned back toward the house, stared at the closed door, and imagined her family sleeping safely in their beds beyond the oaken boards. "I really don't have a choice, do I?" she asked in a quivering voice.

"No," the old man agreed, "you do not. Your pledge was the condition by which this life of yours was allowed. Now you must go, to be there when he blows the horn."

"Let me first get my things," she begged, reaching for the door.

"No!" Argant snapped. "I will not allow you to look upon their sleeping faces. One glance would be enough to break your oath! You leave now!"

Oksana nodded her eyes filled with sadness and loss. She followed the Ancient One into the forest without looking back. Her body would never return, despite her heart remained with her family.

Pulled once more away, Briaca now stood beside Goro, watching from the woods as Argant led Mother away. Tears filled the girl's eyes as her mother departed.

"Where did he take her?" she demanded.

"He took her to Mount Sapientia, to the home of dragonkind, and forced her to take a new form."

"I don't understand."

"Your mother was not fully of human blood, child. She was the result of the Ancient One's ability to blend in with humans. He took many mates in this form, breeding more and more half-breed children like Oksana, through which he hoped to infiltrate and wage war against us vampure."

"Mother wasn't a dragon!" Briaca protested.

"No, but she had dragon blood and it passed into you."

"But why? Why would Argant do such a thing? I refuse to believe you!"

"It has long been understood that the war between the Keryx would end if one of us could figure out how to blend our species. By blending human blood with his, he hopes to turn your brother into his weapon, to kill you and eventually every vampure sharing my bloodline. He hopes to use his brother to kill *me*!"

"Maybe he should!" Briaca resisted his charm. "You're evil! You sent Lars to raid Cardac!"

"I sent Lars to *save* Cardac and the rest of Gaul." Goro argued. "Now that King Chilperic is dead, I will raise Eduard as my vassal and give Cardac to Lars. It is time for feudalism so that all people will enjoy prosperity, just as Titus once believed was *his* destiny to do the same. I owe it to *him* to bring that dream to reality. Think of it! No one will ever hunger, nor will they lust for riches! I have created a better system than I had with the Romans, one that truly equalizes all people of this world. You will take part in this new world. Just as I chose Titus, you too will serve."

"I won't!" she protested. "I refuse!"

"You will change your mind very soon. My sanguis already courses through your veins. Your blood is of my blood, your mind is of my mind, and your actions are ordained by my hand. You are my weapon, my tool, and an extension of my grace. Our sanguis is one!"

Briaca felt her struggle end as death overcame her life. The vision and the room around her blurred into nothing as she entered the abyss of death.

Interlude:
Sanguis

Dominus Titus Aurelius purveyed his province from the window of a bouncing carriage. He had grown to resent the assignment; ten years was too long for a Roman to spend so far from home. These mountains, with their splendid waterfalls and frozen peaks, only added to his irritation. He missed the concrete, the sounds and smells of the city, and the bustling activity of progress. Here in Helvetia, Titus had found more scenery than success.

But his lord had demanded loyalty, insisting this assignment held great importance for their kind. Goro desired to bring an end to the war, to finally settle the dispute over who ruled the civilized world—dragons or vampure. So far the Lord of Blood enjoyed an upper hand. Hunted to near extinction, dragons rarely ventured from hiding while vampure ruled the civilized world. What kind of victory forced the victor to rule from shadows?

Someday, Titus and his kind would wear their forms among society.

The eyes of the dominus scanned those frozen peaks. High and forbidding, they seemed to laugh at his incompetency. In ten years he had not found a single trace of the dragon thunder, the home of Argant, the Lord of Fire, and his descendants. Goro insisted it was there—a mythical roost known only to the locals as Mount Sapientia. It could only be reached, according to legend, by a hero fated to bond with an aerouant through noble deeds.

If I can't find them, Titus realized, *I must draw them out.* But luring a random dragon from hiding would not do. He must find Argant and crush the thunder by severing the head of their bloodline.

The carriage slowed and Titus turned his gaze toward the village ahead. Nestled in a dense forest, Cardac could fuel the empire's war machine, but Goro had forbidden such an industry here, so close to the hidden thunder, and so the land lay useless. The only clearing the villagers farmed paid tribute to the empire, their measly payment to keep the Romans from interfering with their quaint and meaningless lives.

A forced cheer erupted from the village center as a dozen or so families celebrated the arrival of their overseer. They anticipated his arrival with as much eagerness as he felt in coming, a necessary business in which both sides must fake their part. Titus scoffed at the dirt which coated their bodies, clothing, and lives.

Let's get this over with, he thought as the carriage rolled to a stop.

Several children pressed forward for a closer look at their lord, but Marius, the captain of Titus' honor guard gently pushed them back. Only the mayor was allowed to approach the dominus and did so with a prepared speech that butchered the noble Latin.

"Dominus Titus, esteemed representative of Caesar, the people of Cardac welcome you with grace, dignity, and humble loyalty. May your visit strengthen our hearts as well as the empire!"

Weak cheers erupted from the crowd, prompted by applause from those few villagers who understood the words. Mumblings of translation whispered in Gaulish drew some late claps and a few lingering hurrahs.

Titus groaned as the door opened and Marius offered a hand. He ignored it, emerging with a smile and waving enthusiastically at the crowd. He would play his role as a curiosity, spend one night in the village, and then be on his way to the Roman capital of Aventicum come sunup.

The mayor bowed deeply, his foot sliding in the dirt and causing him to stagger awkwardly. "We have prepared a feast, Dominus, in your honor!"

Titus kept his outward smile, still scowling only on the inside. The meal would no doubt revolve around venison or pork, the fare of paupers and farmers. Whatever it turned out to be, it would be more than most of these families had eaten all year. He glanced once more at those laughing peaks high overhead, hoping Goro appreciated the sacrifices made by his most loyal subject.

"Lead me to this feast!" Titus bade the politician, then followed him beneath a covered awning and inside the meeting lodge. It reeked of poverty. Torches flickered above rows of benches alongside table-tops. None of the wood had been polished, soaked and swollen by decades of spilled beverages. Even the grungy walls gave off a musty air that threatened nights of lingering coughs.

Titus took his seat of honor at the head, the mayor choosing a simple chair that sat him beneath the shoulder of the overseer. One by one the villagers entered and took their seats, leading salivating children who eyed the boar resting on a platter before the Roman. Beside that beast also lay the haunches of a hart. At least the back-strap would be saved for their visitor, and a beautiful woman bowed shyly as she placed that platter before the dominus.

He nodded his thanks but remained careful not to eye her as hungrily as he should the meat. The same ritual occurred in every village, them choosing the loveliest of their maidens to wait on his every need. The audacity of their assumptions, that he, a *Roman*, would find pleasure in such an unwashed and uncultured specimen. Titus would never lay beside a Gaul, not when a true Roman woman, Diana, his official courtesan, waited with dignified upbringing in Aventicum.

Captain Marius, it seemed, took no such distinction or pride in his own selection, and showed great interest in the serving girl. Once she realized the dominus had no interest, she seemed content to accept the advances of his guardsman. Titus shrugged. *To each his own taste*, he supposed.

Thus the meal droned on, stretching the evening into a night filled with local songs and stories. He tried so hard not to appear disinterested, only yawning once or twice during a biased and largely unfactual account of the Battle of Alesia. Instead of the arduous siege fashioned by Julius Caesar, these boasts hinted at acts of valor and heroism on the part of Vercingetorix and his Arverni.

Sensing his disinterest, the mayor called upon a young woman to stand. "Adelia!" the mayor begged. "Excite us with a tale about dragons! Come now! Take the floor!"

The next storyteller greatly surprised the dominus. She was a young mother of two children, wife to a farmer by the look of her shabby clothing, but had a different look to her than these other Gauls. While most were tall, fair skinned, and with reddish hair. This woman more resembled a natural citizen of the empire. With smiling brown eyes that matched her bronze skin, a cascade of raven hair framed what could only be a Roman face. Her perfectly slanted nose sloped between high cheekbones and rested above full lips.

Titus watched her with keen interest but carefully guarded the lust which leapt inside with quickened pulse.

Adelia stood, blushing deeply and looking to her husband for his approval.

"I'm so sorry, Erwan!" the mayor added, realizing his unintended slight upon her husband's honor. "Would it please you if your wife entertains the dominus? The decision is yours, of course!"

The farmer, the usual type with a strong back but seemingly lacking the intelligence of his wife, frowned at being put on the spot. Thankfully, her children interceded for the audience. "Please, Father!" they begged. "Let her tell a story about the dragons!"

"Hush now Rupert and Racinda," the young mother cautioned her children. "The decision is entirely up to your father and you shouldn't interfere." She locked eyes with Erwan and gave the slightest of nods, letting him know she would not be bothered by the public attention.

The farmer turned to face the guest of honor and bowed deeply before Titus. "Very well, my lord! I pray my wife's story brings you as much pleasure as it does our humble village."

The entire assemblage relaxed but watched with bated excitement. The hush fell upon everyone, even Titus, as the woman's soft and supple lips curled and spoke her tale of dragons.

"Mount Sapientia," she described, masterfully blending her Gaulish with the correct pronunciation of the Latin name, "blew cold with the air of defeat. The Elderkin, exhausted from warfare, led their children into hiding. Their foe, the evil vampure, had bitten at their heels for eons and sucked their resolve if not their sanguis."

Titus sat taller in his chair, entranced by her telling but also by the details no human should know. She was special, this storyteller, and he would hear her story in entirety.

"Weary from running, they faced the army bearing down upon them. The mountains provided protection, causing swirling winds that prevented the vampure from following them by air. And so their enemy scaled the sheer rocks leading upward, a mass of vampure and voltur intent on feeding upon every drop of dragon blood. The Ancient One, the original of his kind, led the counter attack, a desperate stand by dragons against their evil foe."

Titus sat bewildered by her accurate telling of what could only be of the Forgotten Legion. Goro had sent them in pursuit of Argant the Ancient, the Keryx Lord of Fire. They had chased the dragonkind for days but never returned as either victors or losers. The entire army had been lost, assumed dead and devoured by the last bastion upon the lost Mount Sapientia.

Adelia continued, "The Ancient One attacked not only the vampure, but the mountain itself, melting and crushing rocks with his dragon fire and thunderous tail. As the cliffside fell, so too did his enemy. One by one the vampurekind struck the ground. The dragons decreed that no vampure must ever find their new home and cleansed the base of Mount Sapientia with their flame. Now only the noblest of heroes will ever recognize the trail, and only the boldest will attempt to seek discourse with the dragons.

"The Ancient One prophesied one such hero would someday venture forth to bond an aerouant, the boldest of all humans seeking to give his life over as a vinculum to the Ancient One himself. Through their connection they would strengthen the sanguis and bring forth on this land the strongest dragon ever born. In that form, aerouants would blend with humans, just as vampure and voltur lurk among us today."

The villagers applauded wildly upon the conclusion of her story, and Adelia humbly returned to her seat, nestling into the loving arms of her husband. Erwan grinned at his wife while little Rupert and Racinda, emboldened by their mother's tale, stared into the torches and imagined dragons dancing in the flames.

Titus never took his eyes off the woman, staring deep into her soul and wondering how this story had come to her. She turned once, meeting his gaze, and nervously lost her smile. Her eyes, illuminated by the firelight, had turned golden with fiery sparks dancing within. She turned and whispered to her husband who nodded. Together they stood, gathering the children, and made swift well wishes before departing.

The dominus watched them leave, the cackling laughter of Goro echoing through the Roman's mind. He would no longer depart this village at first light but would wait until the men labored in the fields. Then he would visit this woman, whom he now recognized as a daughter of the Ancient One.

It wasn't until noon when Dominus Titus and his guard approached the cottage hidden deep in the wood. The mayor, emboldened by his delayed departure, had insisted on showing the overseer his ledgers. Duty-bound to act the part of a true dominus, he served his emperor by placating the demand.

Shining splendidly in the sunlight, his gilded carriage arrived outside the shabbiest shelter this Roman had ever seen. It was a wonder the cottage kept out any elements at all, a mere log cabin much too small for the family to which it belonged.

He called over his captain still astride his mount. "Marius, ensure I'm not interrupted, no matter what happens."

"Yes, Dominus," the captain promised.

Just to be sure, Titus whispered, "All your men present, they are of like blood, are they not?"

"They would not have travelled with us, were they not, Dominus." The captain saluted and ordered the guard to fan out, forming a perimeter. Titus approached the only door of the hovel.

Adelia had recognized her visitor through a single window, its shutters open to air the inside, and met him before he knocked. Hiding within, her voice quaked with fear. "Lord Dominus?" she asked in perfect Latin. "You honor us with your presence, but my husband Erwan is not home."

"I did not come for your husband, Adelia. I came to speak to *you*."

"My lord, I can't imagine why. I am the wife to a farmer and have no conversation to offer. If you came for more, I must warn you that my children are playing nearby and will return. I do not wish them to see their mother defiled."

Titus laughed. "I've no interest in your body, only in your stories. I have many questions only you can answer."

"And if I don't welcome you in?"

"I think we both know that wouldn't matter."

Adelia nodded, opening the door the rest of the way. After he entered, she left it open and hanging on its hinges.

She's certainly no fool, Titus recognized, *and also a woman of honor.* He sat in the only chair in the room, a creaking rocker crafted by a farmer's hand. Adelia sat across the room upon the hearth, smoothing her skirt nervously and waited for him to speak.

"Where did you hear that tale, the one you regaled us with last night?" the dominus kindly demanded.

"It was told to me when I was young. By my father."

"Why did you tell it in my presence?" His eyes flashed red, two bloody pools swimming in reflected daylight.

Adelia would have recoiled had she not already suspected his bloodline and recognized him already a vampure. In a calm voice she replied, "Because I did not realize at first you are infectus."

"Infectus?" Titus shook his head at her ignorance. "I assure you I am not the tainted one among us. I believe the term you meant is *donatus*, for I was gifted with my bloodline from Goro himself."

The dominus eyed this creature closely, never having imagined he would come across a dragon in its first form. Her skin, her teeth, her hair, all of it appeared so *human*. But that was the way of all descendants of the Keryx, those spiritual beings after whom humans were fashioned to imitate.

"Hold out your hand," he commanded Adelia.

At first she refused but, knowing she was trapped, finally reached out.

Titus took it in his, rubbing and feeling, then held her skin to the light. It only *appeared* human to the eye. Now that he knew what to look for, the Roman recognized the tiniest of dragon scales linked together with fine blonde hairs sticking up between each ridge.

"Remarkable!" he whispered. "You are one of their infants, a *first* form Firekin!"

"What will you do with me?" Adelia asked defiantly.

"I'm not sure. I've not come across one like *you* before."

"How?" she asked. "How did you recognize my form?"

"I didn't, not at first. You are so rare... I believe your kind are only birthed once or twice in a century. You have lingered long in this form," Titus pointed out, "and should have chosen your adolescent state long ago. Why did you keep this one? Were you sent among humankind to spread your stories? Those lies you told last night were certainly concocted *of* dragons *by* dragons."

Adelia looked away, her eyes darting to the door. Sounds of laughing children approached the cottage but abruptly stopped upon seeing the soldiers. She opened her mouth to scream, to warn them to run away, but Titus had left his chair. In a blur of speed, he had crossed the room and placed his hand firmly against her mouth.

"Of course!" he whispered. "Your husband must be of the same bloodline. Argant sent you here, to hide your species among humans, bearing future generations more quickly."

Adelia did not answer.

"Yes, it makes perfect sense. Dragons procreate too slowly, but your younger form so closely resembles humans. That means your children are like both of you and will someday soon make more and more, blending with humans until your filth litters the human race."

The woman's eyes pleaded mercy for the children, silently affirming his theory, and asked nothing for herself.

Titus looked out the door, holding her firmly in his grasp as he called out in a perfect mimicry of their mother's voice. "Come inside, children!" he lured them. "Come and meet our visitor!"

Adelia tried to get away but Titus had the strength of seven men. Though she could have been stronger, she had remained in this form far too long. She had not trained her muscles the way she should have.

"It *is* about the children, isn't it?" Titus reasoned his thoughts out loud. "Argant's prophecy, about a worthy human, it can't come true unless your children mix their blood. He meant *their* descendants to provide this vinculum, and so he sent you here to birth them." He grinned at the Ancient One's audacity and quickly formed a plan of his own. "Their blood will be useful to my kind as well, and I intend to make it so."

Adelia struggled against his hold, fearing for her children, but once more failed to budge beneath his strength.

"But that won't do, will it? Not fully, no!" Titus mused, his questioning mind racing like a lunatic. "I must also destroy Argant. I must draw him out so that I can end this war once and for all!"

He pushed her hard into the bedroom, where she landed against the far wall. Her neck hit awkwardly but did not break. The blow with which it struck rendered her dazed, her senses failing as she collapsed in a heap upon the simple farmer's bed.

In a blur of movement Titus fled the room, hiding in the shadow next to the open door. As soon as the children entered he slammed it shut and fell upon them both, alternating his bites upon their tiny necks. He was careful not to drain too much, slathering their wounds with his saliva and ensuring they too would join his bloodline... but first they had to die, to rise again as revenants and be fully within his power.

After he finished, the Roman stood, looking down at the future of his race. These will rise again as hybrids, drawn by insatiable desire to find him in Aventicum, to offer themselves freely to serve his master. He made his way to the bedroom, lustfully eyeing a trail of infantile dragon blood leaking from Adelia's nose. She still lived but barely, and so he would do her a mercy by finishing the job.

He feasted then in what the old vampure describe as bloodlust. It occurs when one of his kind loses themselves among the sanguis. Titus had never experienced it, his stoic mind trained by Roman scholars, but he lost it here on Adelia. Without control he ravaged her body while consuming her lifeforce, completely draining and leaving her to rise again with her children.

I do this only as insult to the Argant, he justified his actions. *I'll turn his grandchildren against him!*

"You there, peasant!" Marius commanded someone outside. "Drop your weapons and stay where you are!"

The sound of hoof beats stamped dirt, letting the dominus know his soldiers had the situation under control.

"Who are you?" a terrified voice demanded. It sounded like Adelia's husband.

"Never mind who we are," one of the honor guard said dismissively. "Lay down your weapons and return the way you've come. Be gone from here!"

"But I..." the newcomer stammered, perplexed by their commands. "I live here!" he protested.

Titus pulled himself off Adelia, his mind less crazed and his belly satiated. It rumbled angrily at the sanguis. He would need days of darkness to fully digest all he had consumed. Rising, he left the room, stepping over the bodies of the sleeping children.

"I will see you soon," he told them. "Come to me when you are ready."

Through the open door he saw that Erwan had arrived home. Surrounded by the honor guard the farmer had decided to fight. Titus' men had obliged.

"Oh, to hell with him!" Marius declared, kicking Erwan hard and striking him to the ground.

Titus walked out of the hovel into daylight, its brightness searing his eyes so soon after consuming the sanguis. The effect would only intensify. He pulled a silken handkerchief from his pocket and wiped his mouth, pulling it away and frowning at how much blood had dripped down his chin and neck. He hated being so sloppy, it was undignified for a Roman.

He tossed the bloody cloth aside.

The dominus held one hand over his eyes to hide the light. His bloodstained teeth showed clear behind his scowl.

Though he hated to waste the sanguis, Titus also could not leave this one alive, nor could he gift this dragon's blood to the lesser forms he led. Goro had not granted him permission to elevate them higher. He had taken a chance by consuming Adelia and the children.

"Deal with him," Titus commanded his knights. "I no longer desire a taste for blood."

Without another word the nobleman stepped aboard the carriage, shutting himself away while the driver readied the horses. He faced a two-day ride to Aventicum.

The dominus panicked, realizing he was trapped in a carriage with open windows. The light streaming in from these no longer bothered only his eyes. As it poured in across his hands, it burned his skin.

His body had begun the absorption, taking in the sanguis and twisting and churning his gut as it sorted out the parts of the blood it needed. The cramping would only last a few hours, but he needed slumber to complete the digestion. This process was always painful for a vampure, but worse when consuming dragon blood.

Adelia and the children were infants who had never changed nor taken another form, he mused, realizing his bounty. Only very few vampure had ever been so lucky to stumble upon such pure sanguis. First and final dragon forms were *always* purest.

A common misconception regarding dragons was the belief they hatched from eggs like reptiles. Through his link with Goro, Titus knew these creatures could also change forms. Like a caterpillar or a moth, they form a chrysalis when ready, sealing their bodies inside while every aspect of their composition changes. Some emerge as wyvern while others may choose a longer, snakelike aerouant. Eventually, they may take on other forms as well, eventually assuming their final form of Elderkin.

Had the pain not come on so strongly, Titus would have told the driver to turn around, to spare the farmer from death and bring him along instead, to be fed on later or given to Goro. He reasoned it was too late, that Marius had already killed him. Hopefully, they had not fed.

He tapped the divider between him and the driver. "Aventicum! Hurry without delay!" he commanded, and the whip cracked as they began moving.

This pain and discomfort was no mere issue with digestion. Titus suddenly realized he needed full privacy.

Given its purity, this sanguis would force him into transformation. By the feel of it, the process had begun already. The light now sizzled on his hands, hot and sharp as his skin began to bubble and split. There was some truth to the legends that vampure are vulnerable to sunlight, but that only affected the change that occurs after drinking pure dragon sanguis. No light can be allowed to interfere with the process. The slightest of radiation, even filtered, could alter, affect, or stop the transformation entirely.

Usually, a vampure would seek out a crypt or sarcophagus to achieve the total darkness they would need. Suddenly, an idea occurred to him and the Roman stood, ripping apart the seat cushions to reach the storage space beneath. Hurriedly, he opened the lid and peered down into the compartment. It was cramped, more so than he preferred, but would provide protection during the two-day ride. He banged hard against the panel to once more alert his driver.

"Do not disturb me at *all*!" he screamed. "No matter what!"

Three knocks answered with the driver's understanding.

Stepping into the compartment he lowered himself inside, pulling the lid shut above him. The darkness soothed his skin, cooling it like a soft breeze. The process had indeed begun. A thin layer of mucus secreted slowly from every pore, forming a second skin which would eventually be his chrysalis.

A two-day ride, he calculated in his mind. Hopefully, that would be enough time.

Heavy knocking woke Titus from his slumber. Though cramped, the tiny space had served him well. He only hoped the transformation had completed. Barely able to move within his sinewy web, he raised one hand and weakly rapped two times, the signal urging caution.

Three more answered from outside—the driver understood.

Several minutes passed followed by the soft bounce of movement. The carriage creaked as it slowly rolled forward. Thankfully, Titus had planned for such an abrupt transformation, but worried his legion would be poorly practiced in their response. If they exposed him to light it could all be ruined in an instant. After a bit more swaying and a few lurching stops, all movement ceased.

"Salvator!" a muffled voice called, a woman's, and Titus felt his anxiety fade. She called him by his title known only to his legion, meaning his vampure had received his carriage.

A few heartbeats later the compartment opened. He flinched against any light which may enter. Thankfully, Diana knew what to do and had received it in the catacombs. She raised the lid slowly and gasped.

Titus again worried something had gone wrong. "How bad?" he asked his courtesan.

"Not bad at all," she whispered. Her hands reached into the compartment, gently ripping the webbing from between his skin and the wooden walls of his prison. She took special care when freeing his shoulders, careful not to harm his wings.

"Is the process complete?" he asked.

She slowly turned his face toward hers. Only the faintest of light revealed her smiling eyes. Tears of joy misted their edges. She ran a finger along the crown of bony protrusions along his hairline and traced steep cheeks down to his long fangs, then replied, "The result is *glorious*, Salvator! Where did you find pure sanguis?"

"In the least likely of places—under our noses in plain sight! They were infants, Diana! Firekin! Their mother, a child of the Ancient One, walking among humans and spreading his prophetic lies."

"Why would he expose one of his own children in such a way?" she asked, shocked by the revelation. "He truly *is* as heartless as he is arrogant!"

"To breed with humans, to water down his bloodline in a desperate move to bond more vinculum!"

"Then Goro is indeed winning this war," Diana realized.

"Yes," Titus agreed. "The Ancient One grasps at straws while we continue to guide civilization toward prosperity. Someday Goro will reward us handsomely for our deeds." A thought came on suddenly, causing him to try and lift his body to look around. He proved too weak and slackened in the arms of his courtesan. "Have they arrived?" he asked her. "Have my voltur brought them as I commanded?"

She shook her head. "No, Salvator, no one had come. Who should I expect?"

"My gift to *you*, Diana. The children you could not carry in your own womb. They will be yours to raise as long as Goro allows us both to live."

"Thank you, my love," she leaned in close and, unbothered by his fangs, kissed him deeply.

As she pulled away Titus asked drowsily, "What time of day is it?"

"A little past noon."

"I need more rest, but there is little time to waste. We must perform the ceremony tonight."

Diana agreed. "Legionaries!" she called. "Lift Salvator and convey him to our rooms."

Two soldiers rushed forward, stepping onto the carriage and reaching into the compartment. Carefully, they braced his arms and pulled him to a standing position. The membrane around his body tore away as they did, slowly revealing two broad and leathery wings. The rest of his body had changed as well, taller and broader, more muscled atop his thicker skeletal frame.

As they eased him down from the steps onto the stone walkway, Titus stretched his wings, giving them a shake.

"Glorious," Diana said again. "You're nearly a visage of Goro himself."

Gentle hands shook Titus awake. With his transformation completed during the carriage ride, he had rested away the afternoon in luxury.

"Titus, awaken, my Salvator!"

His eyes opened to find Diana standing over his bed, radiantly youthful as the day the two had met. Titus smiled. He could not imagine his life without his concubine. She epitomized Roman beauty, stern and strong with a mind to match.

"Come meet our children," she bade him.

Ah! So they have arrived! He let out a soft groan as he stretched, reaching out every limb as he prepared to rise. "Have they settle in?" he asked with a yawn.

"Not yet, but soon."

Another thought struck Titus and his eyes again opened, this time with alarm. "You haven't feasted upon them, have you?" He wouldn't blame her if she had, and she still could in these tender moments of their transformation, but Goro would have strictly forbidden her their perfect blood.

"I await what you give me in the ceremony."

Titus nodded. *Good.* As much love as he felt for this woman, he needed her loyalty more than her body. He threw back the sheets, silk from far away Serica, and rose ready to be dressed. The bones in his head and face had returned to their human form. His wings had also contracted inside his body.

"The boy will feed on you tonight," he said with a smile, revealing the true reward he had brought his mistress. "He will serve me through *you*."

"Oh, Salvator," she said, eyes brimming with tears of joy as she wrapped the under toga around his waist and hips. "I can't believe it's finally happened. I'm now a mother."

"Yes," he agreed absently. After their transformations completed, these would have status in his home but could never be his heirs. These would be heir to something greater than his life as a Roman patrician. These would trace a line for him under Goro.

Diana wrapped his toga, also silken to befit his station and trimmed with the same golden edging as his carriage. The garment was long, and she began the wrap by tucking the first fold beneath the crook of his arm.

A slave entered, a young woman from the Thracian region, bearing fresh water. As she stooped to retrieve the pan from his bedside, Titus gave her an order. "Bring the children and their mother before me," he said without looking at the girl. As soon as she departed, he realized Diana had stopped dressing him, holding the long cloth against her mouth and hiding her expression. "What is it?" he demanded.

"I thought *I* was to be their mother?"

"You are. I simply meant she who birthed them. I have use of her yet." He straightened his back and stared at the far wall, waiting for Diana to resume the dressing.

"Why do you want *her*?" the woman demanded, a hint of jealousy in her tone.

The blow came as soon as the question left her mouth, striking a backhand across her lips. "That's not for *you* to question, concubine!" He ripped the cloth from her hands, hurriedly finishing the final wraps himself.

Diana recovered just before the slave returned, ushering the children into the room. As soon as they entered, the woman curtsied then backed out again, closing the doors for privacy.

"Did you get their names?" Titus asked. "I have already forgotten."

"The boy is Rupert and the girl Racinda," Diana said while rinsing a bit of blood from her mouth.

"Where is their mother?"

"Had you allowed me to finish, I would have told you, no *mother* arrived with the children."

Titus knew at once something had gone wrong after his departure from the farm. "Where is Marius?" he demanded. "Where is the chief of my guard?"

"I did not wish to bother you with this before, Dominus, not while you needed your rest, but Marius did not return. Only one member of your guard escorted the children, and he returned with grave news."

"Impossible..." Titus trailed the word into his thoughts. What had gone wrong? Something surely must have, to have delayed Marius. "That's not like him. Has this other soldier given his report?"

"He awaits in the peristylium, Dominus."

"He *awaits*? How long has he been *waiting*?"

"He arrived an hour or two after you did, accompanying the children. I would have had him wait in the atrium, but he seemed low of class. This one is not an equestrian like Marius. Worse, he is merely an Omicron."

Titus raised his hand, meaning to strike her insolence, but paused when he saw two pairs of bloodshot eyes staring up at him. The effects of his blessing were wearing off, and they would need to consume sanguis very soon. Other than that, they seemed unaffected by their sudden change of surroundings. No doubt they stood listening to Goro speaking in their minds, teaching them the history of their new bloodline.

"Keep them here," he commanded his concubine, then stormed from the bedroom.

The peristylium was an open courtyard in Roman homes, meant to be a relaxing aesthetic to complete the domus, combining the surrounding rows of porches and their columns. But that was in

Rome. In Aventicum, where temperatures were much cooler than along the Mediterranean, the area received little use. Other than to view colorfully potted flowers and carefully cut grasses, this courtyard was best experienced behind glass windows or closed shutters.

Titus stepped outside, immediately recognizing the soldier, but struggled to remember the man's name. "You're freshly turned, are you not?" he demanded. This could still be called a man, even if barely achieving his Omicron form. The only thing lowlier would be a voltur.

The soldier leapt from his chair and dropped to one knee, crossing right arm across his heart in salute "Correct, Salvator. I pledged under the last moon."

Titus eyed the evening sky, thankful the sun had dipped low enough to make this conversation more bearable on his skin. He would still be vulnerable to its light for several more days. "Well, spit it out, then. What went wrong? Where is Marius and the others?"

"We did as you commanded, we beat the farmer until Captain deemed him dead."

Titus listened carefully. *Beat him until* deemed *dead.* "What went wrong?" So much of the story seemed unlike his captain.

The man shrugged. "We dragged him into the forest and left the body where no passerby would stumble upon or suspect trouble within the home."

"You beat him, but no one thought to drain an artery or sever his head?"

This confused the soldier. "I don't understand, Salvator."

"I'm shocked Marius failed to recognize the farmer as dragonkind. Why would Marius have believed a simple beating would have been sufficient?"

The soldier frowned and shrugged. "He was anxious, Dominus, to return to the village one more time."

Titus froze. "He returned to the village?"

"No, Salvator, I did."

"So you didn't wait out the afternoon at the hovel?"

"No sir. The captain had met a girl the night before, a local gal, and wanted another run at her. He arrived just before nightfall, but had forgotten his sword. He sent me to fetch it, gave me his horse to do so, since I'm only of the first centuriate class."

"After you returned what did you find? Where were Marius and the others?"

"He had left the woman a mess, bled her completely drained of sanguis, and didn't bother to hide the body. It was broad daylight and I had to wait around till dark to remove it."

"Impossible! Marius would not give in to bloodlust!" *My captain controls his urges,* Titus thought, ignoring his own primordial release.

"I got back late. By the time I returned to the hovel, Marius and the entire honor guard had been killed, cut into pieces."

"Who did such a thing?"

"The farmer, Salvator, he didn't die. He was tougher, somehow, then we expected. He awakened later, wielding iron and attacked our squad from behind."

"Dragonkind don't use weapons to kill. They don't need to! The practice is beneath them, preferring their teeth and claws." Titus paused. Something in this man's story lacked truthfulness. "How is it," he asked, "that *you* survived when the others did not?"

"By the time I returned, the farmer had buried both children and his wife. He had already gone off somewhere. I had no trail to follow."

"Yet you claim to *know* it was the farmer who killed Marius and the others?"

"Yes, Salvator."

The vampure moved quickly, faster than his guardsman could anticipate, grabbing the centurion's throat with one hand while gripping his stomach with the other. The noble vampure could feel sanguis still bloating this Omicron's digestive organs. "You've feasted," Titus accused. "When?"

"No, Salvator!" the man lied.

"When you went back for Marius' sword, you did not find the woman drained. Marius would never be so sloppy! I think you found her perfectly whole and wasted the afternoon violating my orders, *feasting*, while your comrades died!"

The guilty eyes of the soldier confirmed the accusation. "I'm sorry, Salvator. Please forgive me."

"And when you returned, you were too bloated and sore to fight the farmer, so you watched as he buried the bodies, didn't you? That's how you knew where to find them. Then you waited, watching him to leave instead of finishing the *only* job I left you behind to do."

"You are right, Salvator. I couldn't fight him, not in my condition. I could barely uncover the children, but I did! Then I returned directly here and brought them to you."

"What of their mother? Why didn't you uncover *her*, as well?"

"More iron, Salvator. The farmer buried her with it, and it halted her transformation."

"I see. Despite your weakened state, you managed to bury the girl from the village, dug up both children *and* the mother in the woods? You honored me by hiding all evidence of our existence?"

"Yes, Salvator!"

"What of Marius and my honor guard? Did you have the energy to bury them, or are they exposed, burned all day in the sun and revealing our secrets to the entire village?"

The man's expression, his intense guilt and sudden remorse, confirmed Titus' assumptions. At least he had the truth of it, but now a dragonkind was making his way here and was probably close if not inside the city by now.

"As your Salvator, what is my chief responsibility over my legion?"

"You serve as magistrate, my lord, to reward or judge your legion according to our worthiness, ensuring each form behaves accordingly as noble vampure."

"And you have not acted nobly," the Salvator judged. He twisted his hand just slightly, snapping the neck of his soldier.

The sinner slumped to the ground, a victim to primordial blood-lust. Fate sealed, this guardsman would not die, not from a broken neck. He would be demoted, denied sanguis as his body healed. The Omicron form would stagnate and revert to that of voltur.

Goro's bloodline could not act like savages, killing indiscriminately, feasting without permission, or satiating the lusts of flesh—the most common ways by which lesser forms were demoted. Rarely did a higher form behave so badly, especially among the nobles. All those from Beta to Lambda had achieved their rank by deeds, their worthiness determined by their Salvator.

Of course, it was no crime to kill humans, to drain them once in a while as long as certain rules are followed. But vampure should only do so with careful measure, minimizing the impact on human society. Even worse was to draw notice to the existence of the legion and its leadership. That had only occurred a handful of times in history, and each had been dealt with swiftly.

Titus had not realized Diana had followed him into the courtyard. She ignored the heap at his feet. "Everyone is assembled, Salvator."

"Alert my legion. A dragonkind makes his way here. A young one. I want him captured but not drained. Preserve his blood intact. I intend to gift him to Goro."

"Is he the father of our children?" Diana asked.

"He was, until tonight."

"And their mother?"

"Dead. *You* are their mother."

The concubine smiled broadly. "Your legion awaits their Salvator."

The lunar ceremony would begin the moment the full moon reached apex, marking the night when all of Goro's legions replenished their sanguis. This ritual not only kept them civilized but also loyal to their master through each Salvator. The fact the ceremony revolved around the moon was irrelevant. The bright orb merely signaled that supplies of sanguis would soon go bad if not blessed. It also called the noble vampure to receive their allotted dosage.

The miracle of this ritual focused on the nature of blood itself and how long it could be stored. That of humans turned necrotic after only thirty minutes and coagulation worsened an already difficult digestion. Though dragon lifeforce could be stored longer, it too needed special care. The longest Titus knew of any sanguis lasting, no matter its source, was forty days, but that was during winter months or when ice was available to keep it chilled.

It could be bottled and kept longer by adding a mere drop of Goro's sacrifice.

Normally, to drink the blood of another vampure or voltur brought sickness and death, the highest form of blasphemy. But Goro's sanguis wrote all the rules, the source by which all vampure were turned, and a mere drop of his sanguis preserved the youthfulness and form obtained from dragons. He was the Alpha, the father of his kind, and his blessing purified instead of destroyed.

Goro, he thought. *I must speak to him as soon as I can, to beg his forgiveness.* By consuming pure dragon sanguis, Titus obtained this new form, bringing him closer to his lord but without expressed permission. He was now a Gamma, considered among the noblest of forms second only to the Deltas and the Alpha himself. To obtain a higher form, while doing the master's work, would generally receive no penalty. But failure to reveal the change, to hide it away, would be discovered, earning the same fate as the soldier Titus had condemned in the courtyard.

But first the Salvator must perform the ritual, to tend his legion.

The temple of Goro lay beneath another, a proxy paying homage to the impotent Roman gods. He would reach it through winding passages beneath the city. Titus descended a staircase to his wine cellar, pushing aside a panel and sliding a two-high stack of casks to the side. The casters were heavy, too much so for a human to have opened the secret door. It proved an easy feat for a vampure. On the other side three Omicron legionaries awaited their Salvator, ready to escort him through catacombs.

As Titus and his escorts approached the temple, a bobbing torch rushed to meet them. Its bearer, another legionary, panted breathlessly as he delivered his dire warning. "A bad omen, Dominus! Sentries reported hundreds of stars falling from the sky!"

Titus waved the phenomenon away with his hand, dismissing it as superstition. "Bah," he said. "It's nothing!"

"There were also dragons, my lord! The western horizon, the entire sky, was full of them just a few minutes ago!"

This gave Titus pause. Dragons *were* on their way. "Mere trickery and illusion, but remain on your guard tonight. There may be a lower form, an infant dragon, approaching the city. He may have already arrived. I don't know if his magic is strong enough to affect the mind as a higher form can, but remain vigilant. I have the rest of the legion scouring the city. You four must patrol these tunnels. Don't allow anyone who doesn't share our bloodline to enter, not even if they appear human.

But especially don't allow a dragon, he thought.

The assemblage had already gathered by the time Titus arrived, draped in the same red and gold robes as he. From the next room emerged Diana, holding the hands of little Rupert and Racinda. All three wore flowing white gowns of purity. His concubine nodded and Titus stepped up to the altar, carefully removing the clasp of his hooded robe. Letting it drop to the floor, he looked out at their faces, a mixture of Gaulish and Roman, each staring back patiently.

"Today is a special day," he told them.

"His life to us, our lives for him," they replied in unison.

"We also bring two more into the legion," he added.

"Their lives to us, our lives for you."

Titus reached beneath the altar, drawing out three bottles. These contained dragon sanguis, brought to him a year earlier by the Betas. His supply ran low and hoped more would be delivered before his legion began showing signs of aging. Worse, sickness may set in, making them nearly as vulnerable as humans. He poured these out over the middle of the altar, letting the mixture swirl down thin grooves carved into the top. Soon, it pooled near Titus, awaiting the final blessing.

Diana handed him a fourth bottle, this one containing Goro's sanguis. He poured this slowly.

"Just as you have shed for me and I have shed for you, Goro has shed for all of us. May his sanguis enrich the blood of our enemies, purifying the gift it contains within."

"His life to us, our lives for him," they replied in unison.

Titus chose this moment to transform, to reveal to his legion the new Gamma form he wore. His wings, once strong and wide, opened more broadly, spanning farther than they had ever reached. The bones in his face twisted, forming a circular crown worn only by the Alpha, his Betas, and Gammas. He did not allow his fangs to drop, this ritual was one of humility, and not of wanton thirst.

The assemblage pushed back their hoods one by one until all twelve had exposed their own faces. Each of these changed according to their form.

The Epsilons and Zetas grew ridges on their cheeks and brows, but no horns emerged. Those were reserved for the two spiked Delta or higher. The Thetas grew ridges only on their cheeks. Some, the Lambdas and Kappas, still resembled humans. Those with wings, the Thetas and higher, fanned briefly, then humbly lay them flat below their robes. Everyone but the Kappas and Lambdas grew taller and their limbs stretched longer.

After he finished pouring, Diana handed Titus an empty chalice, golden with the Lord of Blood carved onto the side. He held it low against the altar, beneath where the liquid pooled, and pressed a button with his palm. A tiny slot depressed and much of the mixture poured like a tap into the goblet. As soon as it was filled, he released the pressure on the button and the flow stopped.

He held the filled chalice up so all could see.

"Through his blessing and the blood of our enemies, I receive the Lord of Blood."

"His life to us, our lives for him," the congregation replied in unison.

Titus drank deeply, filling his belly with his Salvator's share. Then he leaned his palm once more against the altar and refilled it, stepping around to face the onlookers. He scanned their faces, judging their patience. No fangs had been bared. Stealing a glance at Diana and the children, he could tell that they, too, had not yet given in to the blood lust.

"Come Epsilon and Zeta, fill your belly with your lord," he said.

Two of the communicants, Legate Vulcan Sylla and a visitor, Senator Crius Glaber, stepped out of the first row and drank their ration before returning to their seats. Only then did Diana approach, a Zeta in her own right, but subservient to these two chosen by Goro. She drank what remained and stood once more beside the children.

Titus refilled the chalice and called for the next to be blessed. "Come Theta, fill your belly with your lord," he repeated.

Four members of the congregation stepped forward, lining up for their turns. Among these the Salvator recognized the Gaulish emissary, Urien Yannick, the representative among the non-Romans in the city. Why Goro wished this man elevated to Theta was not for Titus to question, but watching him closely for deviance was a duty he performed with diligence. He did not like this Gaul.

After all Theta had seated, he filled the cup once more. "Come Kappa and Lambda," he said, loudly for those standing in the back, "fill your belly with your lord."

The remaining six robed figures stepped forward, taking their measured allowance according to their ordered rank. Only enough sanguis remained to fill one more goblet, but he set the chalice aside. Holding an empty bottle against the altar, he pressed the button, filling it and sealing the top. This would be served later to his most loyal legionaries—added to a *human* sacrifice on the new moon.

He handed the bottle and chalice to Diana, then motioned for her and Rupert to depart. She would feed the boy a portion of her sanguis, sealing their bond as mother and son. Titus would do the same with Racinda. That would awaken their bloodlust, completing their transformation as a privileged, but not yet noble, Omicron.

He grabbed Racinda and lifted her by the armpits, gently laying her body across the altar.

"It is time for a sacrifice," Titus explained to his legion, pulling a silken cord, dyed crimson, from his robes. He used this to symbolically bind the girl to the altar. He looked into her face as he tied the knots. She still did not realize where she was. Goro still spoke in her mind, his blessing hidden in the saliva Titus had injected when first he fed.

"Blessed is the Life Bringer!" Titus said to the congregation, and everyone in attendance knelt before the sacrifice.

"Life Bringer," the legion sang in return, "bless us with longevity."

Dominus Titus placed his left wrist beside Racinda's mouth, gripping the altar with his right. He spread his wings as wide as they would go, his shadow flickering against the farthest wall.

"May this sacrifice be pleasing," the worshippers sang in unison, "a gift from your chosen few."

Titus scanned the room, marveling for a moment at how much his shadow resembled that belonging to the Lord of Blood. He was a Gamma, a true visage of Goro. "Our lord finds it pleasing," he intoned, "and blesses all his children with eternal youth." He leaned over and opened his mouth wide.

"Her life to us, our lives for you," his legion chanted the words of subservience. Racinda herself would recite them soon, after drinking of his sanguis.

Her fangs finally emerged, as small as they were, and she turned toward his wrist instinctively. She still hesitated, he realized, to bite. Titus felt the surging anticipation of Goro's power pulse his veins, eager to enter the girl. Unable to control his own fangs any longer, they descended as those of a true Gamma, as sharp as his master's.

Titus leaned close and gently kissed the girl's cheek, then whispered, "Take nourishment from my veins," he encouraged, "and rise up as my daughter."

The girl's head turned and she bit, gently at first, but then her eyes closed as the need for satiation took over her mind. This first taste would burn her belly and she flinched with pain as the sanguis entered. Her eyes again opened, unseeing the crowd looking on. It was then, during that brief moment, she found pleasure in her blessing and became Titus' daughter.

"Racinda!" a man's voice screamed from the far entrance. Standing beneath his shadow was the farmer, the husband of Adelia.

Every head in the cavern turned to watch the intruder, pushing back their hoods and baring fangs upon finding a human.

No, Titus thought, this is no human. He is dragonkind like his wife and children! Goro will be pleased by how I lured him into the open. Titus pulled his wrist away from Racinda. She had drunk enough, and quickly untied her bonds.

Hate filled the farmer, driving him forward with a flashing blade in his hand. It was a scythe, the tool of a farmer, most likely the only weapon this man owned. Lost in blind rage, the intruder reaped the nearest worshipers, killing several Kappas and Lambdas and one Theta. Blindly the farmer sliced, his eyes locked on Dominus Titus. He struck down any vampure who dared step into his way. In all he killed six with his iron tool, cutting the noble portion of Titus' legion in half.

The rest leaped on him together, clawing at a dragon scale collar around his neck and biting at his skin.

No! Titus realized this was wrong, watching them attack the gift he hoped to give Goro. As Salvator, he could not allow them to drink from this pure dragonkind, especially not so soon after receiving their blessing. "Do not consume his sanguis!" he bellowed from the altar. "Hold him there!"

To his relief they obeyed, gripping the farmer tightly and holding him to the ground. Urien Yannick, the Gaulish representative, reached down and ripped the scythe from his hand, flinging it aside with a sizzling cry.

"Iron!" Urien screamed. Titus understood his pain, it would scar his palm, especially while steaming with vampure blood. The farmer grinned, eager to deal more of the same.

"Move aside," Titus growled. He had scooped up Racinda, setting her feet on the ground, and now led her by the hand. "Who is this man to you?" he asked her.

"He was my father," she replied dryly, without any bit of emotion in her voice.

"*Was* your father," Titus agreed. "Farmer, what is your name?"

"I am Erwan and *she* is Racinda, but... I don't understand. How are you alive, my dear? I found you and Rupert *bled out* by this beast!"

"Rupert..." Titus considered, "Ah yes. The boy. That *was* his name." *It will be changed to Titus soon.* Turning to Urien, he commanded, "fetch the boy."

"Yes, fetch him and hand my children over to me," Erwan demanded, "and we'll be leaving."

Titus laughed. Never before had he heard such daring from someone about to die. "My," he said, "aren't you a *bold* one. Erwan the Bold it will be. But no, I'm very sorry, you've discovered our secret and killed quite a few of my noble families. They will need replacing." The Roman leaned forward, removing the collar, sniffing and breathing close to the farmer's neck. This man reeked of dragon.

"My daughter," Erwan begged, "don't you want to leave with me?" Of course Racinda said nothing, she had tasted sanguis and now understood the truth of the world as Goro had taught her. "Why don't you stop him?" the farmer asked his former daughter. "Draw the dagger from his side and use it. Help me, daughter."

"I don't want to help you," she answered. "I'm too hungry!" She abruptly lunged, pushing past her new father with bared fangs, biting wildly for Erwan's neck.

Titus reached out a hand, grabbing his daughter's neck and stopping her mid-bite just before making contact. "No. Do not taint your palate with *his* blood." If she consumed dragon sanguis now, it might confuse the transformation. It might even undo the process entirely. *But it also may enhance it!*

Urien returned with Rupert and Diana, and Titus watched as they entered the cavern. The boy licked his lips wildly, snapping and biting the air between him and his father on the ground. His meal had been interrupted.

Erwan turned an angry head, staring directly into Titus' eyes. "Where is Adelia?" he demanded. "Where is my wife?"

"Something isn't right," Titus realized.

This man smelled entirely wrong. The blood within him was not like Adelia's, nor was it like the children's before they turned. Titus told him so. "Your blood is *different* than your children!" He breathed deep against Erwan's neck and added, "They only took after their mother." He sniffed once more then recoiled. Behind his fangs Titus frowned. This man only smelled like dragonkind because he had recently been near one. A *large* one. "You are fully human and only *reek* of dragon! You've been around their forms!" He sniffed again, "Elderkin most recently!"

"My wife is *also* human," Erwan said, his ignorance now laughable. The man had not known!

"She is of dragonkind, and that's why I called your children to me, to drink of my blood and transform. They have chosen a new form, a mix between two Keryx, and far nobler than any single vampure or dragon! They have *chosen* to serve Goro! Now, I will raise them as nobility, granting them a better life than you ever could."

"You are full of lies and deceit! My wife is as human as them and me! Where is she? I will ask her myself."

"Adelia is dead where you buried her. She could not be raised because of the trinkets of iron you left in her grave!" the vampure snapped. "Now answer me, Erwan the Bold, how is it I smell dragon on your body? What is this form you have taken?"

"I am not of their blood and this is no form. I am merely a vinculum."

Titus looked up, suddenly very worried for the legion he tended. He eyed the entrance to the sanctuary warily. "You are bonded? If so, you are the first to do so in a thousand years!"

"My lord!" Urien remarked with excitement. "If he has brought his dragon here, we should feast on its sanguis and our youthful blessings will last decades!"

No, Titus knew that was the last thing his people should do. He wavered, very concerned about what was about to happen. "I smelled Elderkin," he said. "What is the name of the aerouant you have bonded?"

The farmer smiled. "His name is Argant!"

Everyone in the room gasped. Whispers of *pure blood* and *greatness* rippled through the assemblage. Urien cried out, "Argant is the oldest, the first! He is the Lord of Fire! If we drink from a Keryx our blessings will endure *immortality* rivaling only Goro's!"

"You fools," Titus warned without taking his eyes from the tunnel. "None of you can match Argant in your present forms! Nor do you have permission from Goro to do so!"

As if in agreement, a mighty roar echoed down the tunnel and into the sanctuary. The walls shook and torches flickered.

Greedy for the sanguis, the six vampure holding Erwan released him, sprinting from the sanctuary with all the others.

Still atop the farmer, Titus watched them leave, shaking his head at their foolishness. "You all rush to your deaths!" he called out, then returned his eyes to Erwan. "How are you not bonded to an aerouant instead? Why did Argant leave the safety of Mount Sapientia?" He paused, not waiting for an answer and worriedly added, "And why did he send you to face me alone?"

"He's helping me to slay *you,*" Erwan spat, "and then I'll give him the means to defeat Goro!"

Titus again eyed the tunnel through which his followers had foolishly rushed. Shouts and screams now echoed through the catacombs, mixing with an angry dragon's roar. He pulled his eyes away, unable to stomach the carnage their foolishness had rushed into. He looked instead on his concubine, made more beautiful while holding the hands of their children.

She seemed eager to flee and so now did the Salvator. It would be understandable if they did. Goro would understand that not even a Delta could fell an Elderkin by himself.

But I'm no longer a Delta, Titus realized. *I'm a Gamma!* He shifted his weight just slightly as he considered how best to end this human and face the dragon.

But Erwan abruptly pushed, sending the vampure rolling to the side. As the Salvator toppled, Racinda let go of Diana's hand and lunged forward. Her fangs barely missed Erwan's neck, just as his hand drew the dagger from Titus' belt. While her momentum carried her past, he plunged the blade forward, aiming between the Roman's ribs.

He let out a gasp, a silent scream as the blade struck his side, but that gasp quickly turned to laughter as the blade shattered into pieces.

Erwan stared at the useless hilt in his hand.

Titus found his balance and rose to his knees, shoving Erwan away like the nuisance he was, sending him skidding across the sanctuary. The Gamma stood over the fallen man, flanked on both sides by Rupert and Racinda. They had not yet mastered the discipline to control their blood lust, and hunger was all that drove them. Both lunged.

Erwan eyed the discarded scythe laying outside of his reach. He would never be able to reach and use it against Titus. His human reflexes were too slow.

The children reached him, clawing at his neck. It took all his strength to hold them at arm's length, snapping and biting and driven only by their need for satiation. Tears clouded the father's eyes as he stared at the discarded scythe. He would have to release one of his children to grab it and looked between them as if deciding who. The other would be upon him the moment he did.

Erwan made his decision, letting go of both and rolling out of the way toward the scythe. The children clamored and fell, each pulling the other away like drowning swimmers desperate for air. While they fought, Erwan moved out of their reach, away from instead of toward Titus.

This confused the Roman. What was this man waiting for? His dragon? The children would kill him soon.

What Erwan did shocked Dominus Titus. It was something no father should have ever been able to do. He swung the iron two times, once for each of his children, severing their heads and leaving them to roll on the floor.

Even Diana was too shocked to either move or scream. She merely trembled, tears welling up in her throat but refusing to come out.

"You idiot!" An Elderkin bellowed as he lumbered into the room. This was surely Argant the Ancient, the Lord of Fire and nemesis of Goro. "They had not fully changed and could have been cured by *my* blood! That's the reason I let you go ahead, for you to sacrifice yourself so that *they* could be our future! You just squandered your last opportunity to live out your days as their father!"

Erwan, upon hearing the dragon's words fell to his knees beside the bodies of his children.

Titus stared up at the massive Elderkin, slowly reasoning out the dragon's plan. "You sent your child into the human world, hoping she would give birth in that form, producing mixed-breed dragon-humans you could someday use against us? You *wanted* them to be turned vampure, so that you could intervene at the last moment when their minds had not yet accepted their new form. You hoped they would become *hybrids,* just as Goro had sought to create for so long?"

Erwan heard these words and looked up at the Elderkin. "Is this true?" he demanded.

The dragon moved clumsily, his belly swollen from so many devoured vampure. He let out a long and rumbling burp, his fire surging brightly and lighting the sanctuary, then made his way toward Titus, growling and hissing fire as the vampure backed away.

"You astound me, Erwan the Brash!" Argant said without taking his eyes from his prey. "What kind of *father* are you? You left alive the very man you sought to kill and instead hacked your own children into pieces!"

"Do *not* evade my question? Is what he said true!" the farmer screamed. "Did you let me come in here alone, hoping I would be bitten? That my own *children* would feed off me? Is *that* the evolution your kind hope to create? To become *hybrids* like Titus says?"

Argant roared again, swinging his broad tail at the ducking Roman. "You pledged me your life when we bonded, so it matters not what I do with your body *or* those of my grandchildren. You had already given up on living!" the dragon accused. "Knowledge they lived would have dampened your vengeance."

Erwan paused, a mixture of remorse and confusion. "I deserved the truth," he argued, eyeing his scythe. Dark blood dripped from the blade to the floor.

Argant snapped at Titus, turning his attention away from the farmer. Long, foul teeth ripped a gash in the vampure's wing, but the Gamma was faster, stepping aside and plunging sharp claws between hard scales. With a heave, two ripped away. The dragon roared angrily, swatting with a massive arm that knocked Titus briefly to the ground. The dragon loomed over him, breathing foul air that stenched the room. Then he bit down, meaning to chomp Titus in two halves.

As the Gamma turned away, he briefly glimpsed another, bolder, act from the human called Erwan. The man pressed the tip of his scythe beneath his breastbone, gripping the handle with both hands. "You may have my form as promised," Erwan yelled, "but Titus will also kill *you* if you take it from me now!"

These words confused Titus, but it worked to turn the dragon's head before his teeth could make contact.

"Not yet!" Argant roared.

Erwan plunged the iron deep, arching it upward into his heart, then slumped immediately to the ground. The bold farmer died with a smile on his face, his thirst for vengeance quenched.

Titus watched the human die, a bold act, his taking of his own life. He had broken the vinculum. Full of rage, the dragon roared, forgetting about the Gamma at his feet. His fangs bit deep into Argant's exposed neck, drinking deeply, taking as much sanguis as he could draw.

Argant should have been able to fight off Dominus Titus. He had expected to finish him off with a single bite. But consuming so many vampure had slowed him, and the vampure sanguis acted like poison within his body.

What once was Erwan blinked two blue eyes, those orbs changing briefly to fire then back to blue. The Elderkin collapsed atop the vampure as Erwan rose upon two feet. Two hands grabbed the wooden handle protruding from his chest, drawing it out with a grunt.

The poison worked quickly to ruin both mind and body of Titus. As his senses dulled he watched in awe as the human rose from the dead. *No, that's* not *the human any longer!* The dying Salvator had not expected such an exchange, had not realized the vinculum provided for a swapping of souls. The Lord of Fire had finally taken human form, exchanged his own for this human. Argant walked toward his former body.

He raised Erwan's scythe above his head, meaning to bring it down on Titus' neck. Then he paused and cocked his head to watch him feed.

Only then did the Gamma, Dominus Titus of Rome, realize his deadly mistake. He had grown too intoxicated by the sanguis, and only just then realized what he drank. Having so recently consumed pure dragon sanguis, his body would not be able to absorb what was now offered by the dragon. So young and naïve in his new form, he had expected to find only that same meal from the Elderkin's flesh, but Argant had intentionally consumed too many vampure.

Titus now consumed the poison of his own kind, and it alone would kill him.

Normally passed quickly by a dragon after eating, Argant had held the vile sanguis in, allowing it to fester and collect in the case of this very scenario. He knew that humans were unpredictable and doubted Erwan would remain true to their agreement.

I've failed you, my lord! Titus felt his conscious fade.

Without swinging the scythe, Argant fulfilled Erwan's final task of vengeance. He had killed Dominus Titus the Gamma.

"Run," Argant told Diana as Titus died, "back to Goro and tell him what has happened here today. Tell him the war is resumed, and that I *will* find him."

Goro's eyes opened, the lid of his sarcophagus pushed aside with a single heave. The air that rushed in reeked of dragon, but it also hung heavy with the stench of dead vampure. He expected to find Dominus Titus had opened the lid, here to grovel and ask forgiveness over his recent transformation to Gamma, but it was his whore who stood over the Lord of Blood.

She was a disheveled mess, no longer proud.

"What do *you* want?" Goro demanded of the woman, closing his eyes and waiting for her to explain the urgency of awakening her god.

"Argant was here, my lord."

Goro's eyes snapped open angrily. His adversary had been so close, so near, yet no one had awakened him sooner to finish what they had begun so man eons before.

"What did my cousin say?" he asked calmly. "I'm assuming he left a message, or he would not have left you alive."

"He said to tell you that the war is resumed, and that he *will* find you."

Goro sat upright in the hollowed out space beneath the altar, looking at the carnage all around. The only death he *didn't* find was of dragonkind. "And yet," he said with a hint of humor clinging to his voice, "he was twenty feet away and could *not* find me."

He stuck out his arm, not because he needed her help to rise, but to force more subservience from this Roman. He hated Romans even more than he hated the Hellenes and, before both of them, the Babylonians. Every great *empire* viewed itself better than all other societies put together.

"Where is Titus?" he demanded.

"Over here, my lord." Diana led him to the body, filled full of sanguis but the wrong kind.

Goro laughed at the cause by which he died. "Argant is tricky, I'll grant him *that*.

Leaning over the body the Lord of Blood fanned his massive wings, pushing Diana aside as he did. Wrapping them around him and Titus for privacy, he used a sharp fingernail to slice a line in his own wrist. He dripped several drops of his sanguis into Titus' open mouth, then healed the cut with a wave of his hand.

"Open your eyes, foolish one!" he commanded the Roman.

Two eyes blinked and then settled on their lord. "I'm sorry, my lord, I..."

"Save it," the master snapped. "Tell me where to find him. Has he returned to Mount Sapientia?"

"No, my lord. He now walks the earth as a human. He traded places with his vinculum, and his dragon form is a revenant."

Goro clicked his tongue, considering. "You've lost your legion, Titus. Take your whore and go ahead of me to Pannonia. Wait for me there."

The wretched lackey nodded vigorously, then scrambled to his feet and took his lover's hand. Together they fled the opposite way the dragon had gone.

Cowards, the Lord of Blood thought with disdain.

Thankfully, he had hundreds more servants like Titus, thousands even, with whom he had entrusted his legions. Whenever one failed a dozen more would step up. He sniffed the air deeply, taking in the odor of his nemesis and archrival. He could *never* forget that scent.

"I accept the terms of our new war," he told the lingering smell of Argant, "and will beat you by your own rules!"

But first he had to find him.

Part II

Chapter Nine

The pain Titus felt in dying coursed Briaca's veins, convulsing her body while fighting against the vile taste of her own kind. On its distant edges she detected a sweet sublime, a hint of what Titus had almost tasted and what Goro smelled on the air. The blood of Argant, Lord of Fire, lurked just out of her reach as well as theirs.

She recognized Argant now, of course, realizing Erwan was a younger version of the storyteller. She had trusted this dragon to take her brother away, and now Kado may even be dead—another pawn in the chess game of gods.

I saw Kado with a dragon. Has he bonded one, then?

"You're almost one of us," Lars said from his chair. His voice sounded stronger, recovered from digesting her sanguis.

She opened her eyes and turned, defiantly meeting his eyes of blood. His ridges were higher and more pronounced, and two spiked horns reached upward from his temples. While she slept, he had transformed. "I'm not like you," she protested. "We won't *ever* be the same."

The vampure shrugged. "You'll be different, that's for sure, but certainly one of us. You're what Racinda and Rupert should have been, the hybrid blend of two Keryx. Goro chose you. You'll be greater than Titus, I heard him tell you so." Lars moved stiffly, sitting up and leaning forward to come closer to Briaca. "You understand now, don't you, that vampure and dragonkind are not only different than humans but also much more so than each other?"

Briaca nodded.

"You can unite our species, perhaps even end this war."

The pain had subsided a bit but her mind still felt numb, fogged by Goro's intrusiveness. "I understand, and I also believed Argant betrayed Goro during the Keryx War. I saw it in his eyes the same way Goro did. I also know he *used* Erwan, set him up to get what he wanted, and is guiltier than the father for killing those children. But I don't know *why* he did either. I assume he had good reasons."

"Good reasons like greed or to satiate his pride? Perhaps he lusts for power? Does it really matter?"

"No. I watched it as if I were there. It wasn't that well planned," Briaca insisted, keeping the conversation going for no other reason except to remain conscious. "Just like in the first war, after Illusion, Beast, and Shadow disappeared into the Corrupted Realm, Fire stood strong alongside Blood. He never betrayed Goro until after Earth and Sea were defeated, and I don't understand why Goro let *him* do all the fighting. It's almost like Goro started the fights then sat back while Argant fought them." They truly felt like *her* memories, and she felt like she and him blurred together in her mind.

That confusion caused her vision to spin.

Lars shook his head. "Argant desired to rule over mankind unopposed. *He* began the war we still fight today."

"I don't believe you. This feeling, these visions, you've either drugged me or confused my mind with magic. Vampure are evil, monsters who cannot walk in the light."

"I see," Lars moved closer, smiling mere inches from Briaca's face. "I've also heard those tales, including the lies which claim we have no reflection and that you have to invite us inside your home or we cannot enter. It's all rubbish, contrived by dragonkind to confuse the humans and turn them against us."

"You're doing a good enough job of that on your own," Briaca pointed out, rubbing her temples while focusing on his eyes, wishing they would cease changing sizes with each pounding thrum of her head. "By stealing away the people of Cardac, you've *proven* your wickedness."

"Again, you're not paying attention. As Goro explained, we are the *benefactors* of humankind. Since they fear us so, we have to operate from behind the scenes. Goro had identified that feudalism is an improvement for all of them as well as us. But humans are stubborn and won't ever accept it on their own. So we have to shake up their lives, shuffle them around, and split them among all villages throughout Gaul. Lord Eduard, now that Chilperic is dead, will rule what is to be named the Burgundian Kingdom."

"Because Goro wills it?"

"Yes, but mostly because the people *need* it."

"And the rest of Gaul in the north?"

"Clovis will rule the Franks."

Briaca felt the room surge, her voice quivering as she asked, "And what of the Goths? Will Alaric be toppled by Goro?"

Lars laughed. "Alaric rules at the *mercy* of Goro, just as Titus and his emperors did. So too, now, does Theodoric in the east. *All* kings rule at Goro's pleasure, just as the Romans did before rejecting his plan for feudalism."

"The Romans are still powerful," Briaca argued.

"Silly girl. They ignored Goro and he *crushed* them instead of forsaking them! When Odoacer sacked their precious city nine years ago, did you not question *how*?"

"Of course not! I was a child!"

"As all humans *are*," Lars agreed. "Rome did not fall by a single event, rather by a series of political decisions arranged, set up, and executed by Goro. He knew that hegemony had run its course. Europe was ready for feudalism. He compelled the emperor to over-expand, making the empire vulnerable to the Huns and Barbarians. He also bribed and bought the Roman government, destroying their economy by encouraging an overreliance on slavery."

"What of the Christians? They won't stand by and allow vampure to take over."

Lars laughed. "Goro controls them too, only differently. He *fanned* the flames that drove Roman Christians into fervor, encouraging the citizens cast aside the Roman gods for theirs. They, too, will serve him nicely as feudalism takes hold, just as Pope Felix serves him now. Once the dust settles, and the people are ready, Goro will choose and crown a Frankish king as the new emperor. The Pope will crown him a *holy* emperor who will unify all of Europe under a single flag of prosperity. It will be glorious!"

"How is it that vampure walk in daylight?" Briaca asked sluggishly. Her mind had reached full inebriation, and it wandered from the conversation. "Why don't you look like Goro? Where is your crown of horns, and why are your wings smaller? How is it you can hide your fangs?" The euphoria of Goro's sanguis now worked to transform her body.

"Vampure have many forms, starting with Goro, the Alpha, down to voltur, the Omega," Lars explained, smiling broadly. "I thought you would have learned that through Titus. You have reached the first level of transformation."

"You're a Delta," she realized from the spiking pair of horns that did not yet crown his head.

"Very good, and you are a Sigma, a transitioning vampure whom I intend to elevate to Lambda or Kappa very soon. That will make you noble, did you realize that? *You,* the daughter of a dirt farmer, will be as noble as the Romans who followed Titus more than four hundred years ago."

"I don't *want* to be noble," she argued.

"So says the best of nobility. Those who want it abuse it, those who refuse it deserve it. Goro taught me that."

"How did *you* turn?"

Lars leaned back, thoughtfully remembering some distant memory. "I started at the bottom. I was turned by voltur but rose above them, worked my way through Omicron to become this form you see today." His voice had softened when talking about himself, as if it pained him much to do so. Perhaps those memories were too painful. He flipped the conversation back to her. "Briaca," he said soothingly. "It's almost time for *you* to take one of these forms. All you have to do is make your choice. Join us in defeating the dragonkind or die alongside them."

Briaca was quickly losing consciousness, she had grown so weak with hunger, and couldn't remember the last time she ate. "That's where you and I differ. I know there are no such things as dragons, they are figments of wild imaginations, stories told by mothers and believed only by children. They exist only as legends."

Lars gently shook his head as if disappointed in his pupil. He also had not bothered changing his form to again appear human. "You will see. One of them is coming *here* tonight with your brother. You were right that I did not need to split up the people of Cardac, not for feudalism to find its roots. They would have followed whatever leader was put over them. No, Goro had me do that to lure out Argant."

"I don't believe you."

"I told you that dragon sanguis courses your body but have not told you *how*. Your mother told those stories every night because she was preparing your brother for his destiny. I saw him earlier today, cloaked in magic as he followed me through Cardac. He has bonded an aerouant, but not just any. This one is special. He will arrive here soon atop her back."

Briaca closed her eyes tightly, fighting back tears as Lars stood to depart.

Kado, she begged her brother, wherever he may be. *Don't come! Stay away from Cardac, Kado! Please!*

Chapter Ten

Briaca had lost all sense of time after Lars departed. Without anyone with whom to talk, to anchor her reality, she plummeted down a shaft of nothingness. No more visions came, no voices conversed in her head, and only the beating of her own heart kept her company.

She focused on its rhythm, a thumping that reminded she clung to life. *But I died,* she realized, the booming of her own thoughts startling the organ and pushing it to pump faster. *Lars killed me, drained me of my blood.*

But the dead do not eat, and the hunger of this girl had grown overwhelming. How could she have died?

An aching rumble shook her belly, twisting, convulsing, and crying out for food.

Briaca had never felt such pain, not even as a child after eating berries in the wood—even after Mother had warned her not to.

Mother. That woman had left, abandoned her children and chose a new life for herself.

Selfishness. The ring of that word stung her heart but soothed her stomach. She remembered Goro had used it to describe dragons, and they are filled with sanguis... sweet, *sweet,* sanguis.

Blood—lifeforce, ichor, nectar. No matter what description it's given, the word invokes feelings of emptiness. Thinking of it drives one to selfishness, to fiercely keep what is theirs and hide it away from the world. It is not to be shown nor set free.

Now, Briaca thought of it differently, imagining it as honey, sweet and decadent, a thing to be prized when obtained. One eats it sparingly when lucky to find the confection, a taste here or there upon toast or as a dab to remove bitterness. Only a child would sneak into a cupboard, tasting from the jar and licking it clean. A child... or a beast like a bear, giving in to wanton urges to rip a hive asunder, licking its comb while ignoring the stings of those fiercely guarding the nectar. That was how Briaca felt when thinking now of sanguis.

Sanguis. The word took special meaning.

Her stomach no longer growled. It roared like a selfish dragon, concerned only for itself, for what it craved, while lacking empathy or compassion for those in way of its needs. Only sanguis would soothe this hunger, this desire, a feeling she could no longer describe.

In her misery she had not realized Lars returned. "Thirst," he had said, accurately describing the feeling now coursing her body.

She rolled toward him, no longer repulsed but comforted by his arrival, and opened her eyes to plead mercy while her mouth still struggled to find words.

The bareness of his wrist met her lips as he bent over reassuringly. "Drink," he told her with a voice of command, like a father would encourage his child to behave.

Oh, how she had tried to please Father after Mother left them, but his commands had been more difficult than this simple word. *Take care of Kado,* he had insisted. *Raise him a man while I'm gone, and teach him the things I would have.* What kind of father walks away from his children? What kind of *mother* abandons?

"I will never go far. Will never leave you," Lars promised, stroking her hair with his free hand. His wrist belonged to Briaca, wrapped by her lips and tasted by a ravenous tongue. "They were wrong to have put so much on your shoulders, too demanding of your abilities and selfishly ignoring your needs."

Briaca could no longer argue any of his words. Only truth was spoken within these walls of her prison—no, not a prison but a cocoon, a place for metamorphic beginnings. The ignorant girl no longer existed, replaced by something stronger, able to obey the commands of her new father. She wanted to please him, *needed* to please him, and right now he wanted her to…

"Drink," he said again.

Her teeth felt the softness of his skin but her tongue only felt the beating of his heart thumping out the same rhythm as her own. This beating also served a reminder of life, but no longer hers alone. They were the same, this man and she, foundlings taken in by another father. One who would never leave them.

Goro spoke into her mind. *Drink, child. Do as your Salvator commands. Like a father he anticipates your needs and provides for them. Give full trust over to him.*

I don't know how, she admitted.

I will guide you, Goro promised.

As soon as he had spoken, a euphoric wash cleansed the young woman's body. Without realizing, her fangs had pierced her Salvator's skin. His sanguis now licked her tongue, wetting her mouth and warming her belly with feelings of contentment. Where it once cramped and twisted against hunger, her stomach relaxed, smoothing out and sending a wave of contentment through her body. As it reached her chest, Briaca shuddered.

This new sensation fanned out, sending pulsing pleasure through every part of her body. Never before had she experienced so much feeling, such exhilaration or pleasing. This was no climax she felt, but a beginning. A basal pleasure gained by giving in to the needs of her body.

"Good," Lars encouraged, "but not too much." She felt him gently pry her mouth away, then felt the warmth of his body move just out of her reach. "Sleep, child, complete your transformation. I will not go far but must bid you goodnight because I must prepare for our enemy's arrival."

Sleep, she reviled the word, having done so much of it in recent days. They had blurred together, driving her to rise from her bed and resume life. She tried and found she could not. Her body was not ready. Briaca succumbed.

This slumber brought dreams of dragons.

Lars felt the cool night wind against his skin, letting it chill the burning desire to satiate overwhelming thirst. That would happen soon, but for now he soared above Cardac. Being winter he should have frozen at this height, but that warming dragon thirst fueled from within. He was a Salvator, entrusted by Goro with lives and had just completed the addition of another into his legion.

Briaca held so much promise, both as a warrior and future lover.

The more time he had spent alongside her had bonded more than their minds. That he had chosen to complete his transformation, locked away with her in that room, surprised him. He normally would have sought out a different place without light, a cubby, a box, or his own sarcophagus. That had been buried deep centuries ago, before he walked the earth among the first occupants of this region. That he had chosen the girl's room, to transform beside her, came as a warm surprise.

But her transformation was not complete. She was still a Sigma. As such, needed guidance from her Salvator.

He had drained her, blessed her veins with Goro's presence with his saliva. And she had reanimated on her own, crawling back from death with the strength to join his legion. Now she has thirsted, drank of his sanguis, and knows well both her Salvator and their mutual master. That meal must settle, but soon she will need to feed again.

Goro had often promised Lars a legion of his own. Finally, after working his way up from Omega and proving his value to the Lord of Blood, his legion would grow. Briaca would be at his side, his hybrid warrior who would help him find and cleanse Mount Sapientia of dragons. But first he must deal with her brother and his monstrosity.

Lars relaxed his body in the air, keeping his wings outstretched while he glided soundlessly, circling the village. Pitch black the night;

he would not see the enemy approach. With eyes tightly closed, he listened and felt for the slightest disturbance of the night.

A dragon is never graceful, not like vampure. They lumber, destroy, and throw their weight around like a mace or battering ram. When they fly it's the same, beating against the air, forcing it to obey, lofting their heavy bodies higher by sheer displacement.

Lars' eyes snapped open as the distinctive thrum of heavy wings struck his cheek. He waited, measuring the dragon's size by its timing and rhythm. This one was not fully grown, an aerouant barely bonded, who dared approach his village.

She neither saw nor heard him coming, too busy talking to the boy. While she scanned the ground for a place to land, Lars gathered speed. He aimed to knock the boy free of his seat and to cripple her right wing as well. He rammed his shoulder into her side, just below the joint of the humerus. The wing immediately folded upon itself and, as he slid up and away, Lars dragged sharp nails across her scaly webbing.

The spin she entered offered no recovery, spiraling downward toward the meeting lodge. As they tore through the thatch roof and crashed into the feasting table, the boy tumbled off and rolled. Two ribs cracked loudly against a wooden beam.

Too bad he hadn't perished, it would have sped the battle.

The aerouant quickly regained her feet, sensing the trap even before Lars' Omicron soldiers rushed to attack. Her long body whipped and thrashed as they stabbed and slashed with spears and swords, forcing her backward into the lodge fire and scattering its embers. One of them pricked a scale, tearing it off and revealing pink tissue beneath.

"There!" one of the men shouted. "It has a wound, attack it there!"

The dragon did her best to protect her weakened armor, turning her body and absorbing their blows with her back.

"No!" the boy, Briaca's brother, cried out. Lars remembered his name as Kado.

Despite his newfound courage, the boy was untrained, unable to fight these larger men. He reached into his satchel and drew out an object. Surprisingly, it was a dragon's tooth, perfectly fashioned into a summoning horn.

Lars descended into the hall, his leathery wings and pointed fangs fully extended. This was a time for showmanship, to terrify the boy and force the dragon to err. "Stop him," he commanded his soldiers, pointing at the boy, "before he summons the others!"

The boy gave the object a pitiful blow just before a boot met his injured ribs. Swift hands gathered the tooth as three more soldiers rushed in.

These did not belong to Lars.

Lars watched with amusement as the pikemen, having seen the dragon fall during their randomly timed approach to the village, raised their weapons and rushed forward, shoulder to shoulder to aid in its killing. "We saw the thing plummet and are here to help!" one of them cried out to those fighting.

But the boy recognized one. "Father!" he called, and his father turned toward his voice.

"Don't worry, we'll save you, son! We saw the dragon attack as we approached the village. Go, now! Run for safety while we help kill it!" the pikeman promised.

"No! The dragon is good, Father! He pointed a finger at Lars, whose hungry fangs smiled back at the boy. "*This* vampure kidnapped Briaca! He has her hidden away!"

"Kado is right! Kill the vampure, Conrad!" the aerouant urged the pikeman.

Confused by the dragon's ability to speak, all three pikemen froze in place, looking between the dragon and the vampure. Conrad especially found himself distracted, blinking uncertainty in the moonlight flooding down from the open ceiling.

Lars almost did not believe the unfolding of this turn of events. He knew the dragon would be their mother, but the arrival of their father added layers of irony. Oh, how he loved irony. The man did not yet understand his wife was not human. He needed more time to piece it all together.

The boy addressed the vampure. "I blew the horn, Lars! What will you do after more dragons arrive than you can possibly defend against?"

"It's too late," Lars explained. "I've already summoned my own legion!"

Kado laughed, the pain piercing his ribcage. "Mother and I *killed* your brood! All of them, each of your voltur are dead. We found them asleep in the tomb beneath the ruins!"

"Lies!" It was Lars' turn to laugh. Such an accusation was impossible. They were hidden well, undisturbed for millennia. The boy was bluffing. He turned to watch his soldiers surround the aerouant, keeping her pinned down by their swords.

"I am *not* lying! Mother and I found them hidden beneath ancient ruins. *Fon talamh tha deamhain.* Beneath the earth lies demons, Lars! And we found them! Mother and I *killed* your legion of demons!"

No, Lars thought, *the dragons have prepped him, told him what to say. There's no way this boy and a single dragon could have killed my legion.*

"Mother?" Kado's father muttered. He looked at his son with confused silence, mouthing the word he did not understand. "Son, your mother left us. She is not here."

"Conrad, help me against these soldiers," the aerouant begged. "We must protect Kado and find Briaca."

Somehow Conrad understood, recognizing his wife's voice despite its rumbling tone. He nodded to his partners, and they reluctantly agreed, stepping up beside the dragon and pushing away the advancing swordsmen.

All eyes watched the scuffle. Even Lars missed Kado when he made his move. The mercenary beside the boy, still gripping the tooth, turned too late, unable to stop him from drawing a long dagger from his own belt. The mercenary let out a gasp as it entered his body, rammed upward beneath his ribs and quickly finding the heart. The tooth tumbled from dying hands and landed on the floor.

It was a bold move, and Lars could not help but admire the tenacity in this boy. After they killed the dragon, perhaps he should turn him as well.

Yes, I believe I will, Lars thought, *and Briaca will help me!*

Kado knelt, grabbing the dragon's tooth and holding it aloft to show it deeply stained with blood. "Look upon this tooth, Lars," the boy commanded. "We found your tomb, smashed your sarcophagus, and killed every last one of your demons! Your brood *is* dead, and so soon shall *you* be."

Lars turned, focused on the blood and smelling it for the first time. The boy had not lied.

Fury filled him, driving the vampure toward Kado with incredible speed. He flew across the room with wings beating fast and arms outstretched. He would do it now, drain him dry and inject the essence of Goro.

The idiot never budged, stupidly holding the dagger with his right hand and the dragon's tooth in his left, facing off his attacker's rampage. Lars had not expected bravery and it confused him. He failed to see the dragon react to protect her vinculum.

Across the room she swung her tail, sending an eruption of embers into the air while sweeping fire, missing the pikemen and striking the Omicrons. As they flung against the wall with a sickening crunch, she moved even faster than Lars, knocking him away from her son, just as he bit down. The vampure rolled into a heap of leathery wings, his breath knocked free, and his mind stunned from the blow.

Lars lay there twisted, looking up at the aerouant looming over his mangled body.

Conrad rushed to his son's side while his pikeman friends flanked the dragon, pointed their weapons at the vampure. "Are you okay?" he asked. "What is going on?"

"I'm fine," Kado told his father, wrapping him in a tight embrace. "But Briaca is missing. This... *thing* took her. But I found Mother and brought her back to help us."

Conrad turned to look upon his wife, now a dragon snarling over a fallen vampure. "Oksana, is it really you?" he asked.

"It is I, Conrad," the aerouant spoke sadly. "I'm sorry I could not tell you before. I had no choice but to leave and now you know why."

"I don't care about why, anymore" the boy's father said, staring up at the beast. "I only wish I understood *how.*"

"I have always been dragonkind," she told him. "My bloodline descended from the Ancient One himself. I'm sorry I could not tell you. I was sworn to secrecy."

"This is all too much," The pikeman wavered, his mind suddenly racing with so many questions, "you swore to be my *wife*, but now you're not even human!"

"It was for our children," she answered. "That is all I can say. I will tell you more, if there is time, but for now I must rid the world of this plague." She leaned low over Lars, cringing as if preparing to eat a rotten morsel.

Lying in her shadow, Lars managed enough strength to raise his head from the ground. He pointed upward at shadows looming above the damaged ceiling. His cavalry had come. From behind a bent fang, he said simply, "You fools. Dragon horns don't only call dragonkind. They also call vampure, letting them know it is time to dine!"

A dark shape fluttered above the open ceiling, cautiously waiting and watching the chaos below. One by one other figures joined the first, lowering themselves into the lodge with leathery wings slowing their arrival. There were six in all.

Lord Eduard's legion had been near enough to hear the horn and responded. Two vampure lunged at the pikemen and two attacked Oksana, biting and tearing at her scales. The others helped Lars to his feet and moved into a defensive position in front of him. He ripped away the mangled fang and tossed it aside, concentrating on moving another down into its place.

The aerouant thrashed against her attackers, biting and beating them back with her head and tail.

"Lord Eduard!" Conrad, his own attacker held back by the long pike, recognized the Delta vampure now attacking the dragon.

The nobleman's sharp teeth frantically bit at her missing scale. "Kill them all," he commanded the others, "then quench your thirst with dragon blood!"

The pikeman gave his own attacker a swift punch to the jaw with the handle of his weapon, spinning and handing him off to his partners. They turned him and their own vampure with a coordinated step, freeing Conrad to attack Lord Eduard. He lunged, intent on protecting the aerouant. The tip of his weapon shattered against the nobleman's back.

The vampure turned and hissed but returned its attention to the dragon. Rearing back, he struck, plunging white fangs deep into the soft underbelly. His body shook with pleasure as he slowly consumed her lifeforce. Try as he may, Conrad could not dislodge the vampure, sucking like a remora from the aerouant.

From across the room, a door opened and another form arrived. A young woman, dressed in simple clothing, stepped into the hall. Briaca had awakened and, though still a Sigma, had nearly completed her transformation. She chose her rightful place beside her Salvator.

Kado recognized his sister at once. "Briaca!" he cried, causing the dragon and one of the pikemen to look away from their attackers.

Chapter Eleven

Briaca took her place beside Lars, watching the commotion that had awakened her from restful slumber. Though hunger had subsided, she felt ready for another meal.

Lars leaned in close, his lips so near to her skin, caressing the marks he had left so many days before with his tongue. She yearned for him to bite down again.

"Would you like to feast?" he asked, sensing her cravings.

Briaca's mouth instantly watered and drool slipped down her chin. Turning to watch as Lord Eduard drank deep from the dragon, she licked a wet tongue across her lips, feeling the fangs in her own mouth, and yearned for dragon's blood. She watched a stream of it flow down the nobleman's chin.

The dragon fought relentlessly, refusing to stop though her strength had noticeably faded. Her fiery eyes had dimmed and weakly watched Briaca.

Two vampure overwhelmed a pair of pikemen, breaking their long weapons in half and pushing them into retreat. The men's eyes filled with terror, appearing ready to flee into the night. Fear locked their feet firmly in place. All at once Lars' companions joined the others, sprinting across the room to feed. The four noble vampure fell upon the pikemen, biting and chewing their lives into submission.

"Briaca, honey, it's me," a third pikeman said, standing beside a young boy. "I'm back from the war," he told her. "I'm home again and we're together."

All she could see of the man was the pulsing vein in his neck, triggering her first blood lust. It overwhelmed the girl, pushing aside all reason as she raced forward, faster than any vampure in the room had yet moved.

She leaped upon him and feasted wildly.

From across the room, the dragon groaned, her fading eyes now paled to a soft yellow. Somehow she found strength, hitting Lord Eduard and the other vampure hard against the wall of the lodge. The heavy logs cracked against the powerful impact, and bits of moonlight trickled in, but neither vampure released their hungry grip. Finished with their pikeman meal, four more rushed to feast on the dragon, their claws ripping away scales to reach the soft, tender flesh underneath.

Briaca did not care. Right now all that mattered was draining this human dry. Lars made no effort to stop her, himself holding back from attacking the dragon. She briefly wondered why.

"She's special," she heard Lars say to the boy. "I just didn't know *how* special she was when I found her. No, that revelation came after I first tasted her sanguis. I have tasted dragon's blood before, but never untainted. They always poison their blood when they know they will be feasted upon, rendering us ill and weakening the effects of the sanguis. She, like you, did not know your mother's lineage."

"You've turned her into a monster," the boy accused, "a hybrid you did not intend."

"Perhaps," Lars said dismissively, "but she empowered me more than I strengthened her. Such a sweet gift she has given through her ignorance, one I believe you will also share with me."

Briaca felt the pikeman heave a final sigh before falling lifeless beneath her body. She looked up from her meal, still lusting for sanguis and rested her eyes on the boy. She and Lars leapt in unison, moving too fast for him to fight back. On each side of his neck they bit deep, drinking fast to satiate their hunger. This was her first taste of dragon sanguis, surprised to find it lurking in the boy. This is why Lars had waited, held himself back from the dragon. This one knew not how to taint his blood.

A shadow passed over the lodge, a large shape, but neither Briaca nor Lars paid it a glance.

"Enough!" a voice bellowed from the doorway. Abruptly, the room fell into full darkness. One heartbeat. Two. Then the room exploded with strobing lights.

Every vampure in the room pulled away from their meals, drunk by their feasting and blinded by the sudden brilliance. Eduard and the others, once noble by birth and position, had been rendered wretched by their feasting. They covered their eyes behind leathery wings and discarded their meals. Having consumed so much of the aerouant, they appeared sluggish and dazed by her poisonous sanguis.

Lars and Briaca released the boy and recoiled immediately, both clear of mind and strengthened by the sanguis. Each stood ready to fight.

Briaca recognized Argant the Old. The ancient storyteller held his dragon bone staff like a fairytale wizard, standing in the doorway with a fierce scowl.

"Enough!" the old man said again.

Another aerouant had arrived. Large and foreboding, it stood just beyond the smaller, dying dragon. He abruptly charged, chomping two vampure in a single bite. He quickly consumed their bodies while Lord Eduard and three others roared displeasure. The dragon held them back with a roar. They held their bellies, bloated and full, staggering with dizziness.

The entire ceiling abruptly ripped away. From the gap emerged the skeletal remains of an ancient dragon, larger than two full-sized aerouants. More than a dozen wyvern flew past this monstrosity, just as full-sized Elderkin peered in with angry, swirling eyes. They had come to not only kill, but to feast upon the now surrounded vampure.

Fast and nimble the aerouant charged the noble lord of Cardac. He tried to fight back but faltered, wracked by the pain in his bloated belly. The dragon moved in for another kill, but Eduard drew a silver sword and plunged it deep into a fiery eye.

The beast roared, his misery emboldening every drunken vampure in the room. They fought against the wyvern with renewed vigor, fierce albeit short-lasting. The mighty aerouant recovered, knocking the sword from the nobleman's hand and sent it flying across the room. Two wyvern grabbed the vampure from behind and tightly held him before their protector. Argant struck quickly, piercing Eduard's chest with a single swipe of his claw.

Argant, full of vigor, grabbed the doorframe with one hand, pushing it wider with inhuman strength. One by one the walls fell, the building itself disappearing. In mere moments, an entire thunder of dragonkind charged the remaining vampure trapped within. Eduard and his legion were torn asunder in a ferocious bloodletting. By the time they had devoured the final piece of vampure flesh, the dragons encircled Briaca. With teeth bared, the beasts snarled and growled.

The boy she had fed upon roused at her feet. She glanced down, finally recognizing him as Kado. Just beyond him lay Father, drained by a vampure. Her knees buckled when she realized which one. She turned, looking for Lars. He had fled during the commotion and was nowhere to be found.

The massive aerouant leaned in and sniffed. "They're infected," he accused. "We should kill them now, and be done with your experiment!"

"Of course they're infected," Argant replied angrily, "as *expected*! I told you this was the way it had to be! In your frenzy to destroy the vampure, you let Lars escape," the old man pointed out. "*That* wasn't part of the *experiment*! Go find him. See if he leads you to Goro. He's tasted pure sanguis twice now and will be closer soon, in form, to his master!"

Argant shoved his way between the elder dragon and the siblings, using his staff to shoo off the others. The aerouant gave a huff and an angry roar, then rose into the sky and began slowly circling the village. All dragonkind in the room gave the storyteller space, all except the animated skeleton. It came closer to examine Kado, tasting the air around the boy.

He stared upward, too intoxicated to protest.

"You'll become like your sister if you don't follow my instruction," Argant explained, his tone full of compassion and a bit of sympathy.

"Unless you do as I say, you will both be cursed by this infection, forever doomed to thirst. The eternal hunger will corrupt your soul and you will live out your days like the vampure."

Briaca knew she should feel remorse for what she had done, but it still felt like the crime had been committed by someone else. Bit by bit the details flooded back, forming a vile lump in her throat.

"Bring them to *me*, Ancient One," a weak voice called out.

Briaca recognized the voice. It sounded like Mother. Then she remembered the conversation to which she had awakened, while Kado shouted to convince Father the dragon was Oksana. That dragon lay still and dying, drained of color as well as life. Then Briaca understood. Lars had warned her, said that she and her brother had dragon's blood, and now she knew it was true. She had tasted her own inside her brother.

Invisible arms squeezed tightly around her and Kado, paralyzing them with unseen magic. Argant's staff nudged each from behind, coaxing them toward their mother's deathbed. She still lay upon the cool embers which had once roared flaming warmth.

"I failed you, Mother, and also Father and Briaca."

"No. You have done well, my son. But now you have a choice. You may give in to the dragon thirst that drives the vampure, or choose to serve your bloodline. It's time, son, to choose your form, just as I chose mine."

"I don't understand."

"When you first found me atop Mount Sapientia, you believed the other aerouants and I to be younglings. Argant told you we were *not* the young, and he told you the truth. We were small because we were unbonded. Dragonkind do have younglings, but not as you would expect. When we hatch from our eggs we have the same form as you. We appear human. Only after we mature and emerge from our first metamorphosis do we appear as dragonkind. I was young when Argant asked me to go into the human world, where I met and fell in love with your father, bore him two human children who could adopt a different form altogether."

"None of this makes sense," Kado insisted again.

"You're dragonkind," Argant snapped, "but no longer like us. You're sanguis is mixed with that of the vampure, and it's time for you to choose your next form. You could emerge as mostly dragon, a hybrid who walks among humans with greater powers, or choose to serve Goro's dragon thirst and take the form of that dark lord. Be warned, his disease flows through your veins, and we must kill you if that is what you'd rather become."

Briaca managed to speak. Her voice quivered like a toddler first balancing on their legs and sounded like she had not spoken for years. "I killed Father," she said, her words neither a statement nor question. She had only just admitted her crime. "There's no hope for me."

"There *is* hope for you," Oksana assured her daughter. "The disease inside you killed Conrad. Just as villagers should not blame any traveler who brings a plague, you shall not be blamed for quenching that hunger before given your choice. True, you drank human sanguis, truer it was your father's, but you have a chance at redemption now, after tasting the sanguis of your brother."

"How?" Kado asked. "I feel it in me too," he admitted, defeated. "How can redemption be possible?"

"By curing the illness," Argant explained, his eyes meeting Briaca's. She shivered beneath his gaze. "Your sister has nearly broken free of its grip, but the disease still holds. There is one way to cleanse you both."

She started to speak, to ask him how that could be true, to demand that what she did be undone.

Kado spoke before she could form the words. "She drank my blood, tasted my sanguis, and that helped her find clarity."

Argant nodded. "You gave her the purity of your blood, and that cleared much of her confusion brought on by the plague. But it isn't enough. You are half human, and therefore your sanguis could not fully cleanse her, could not restore her as dragonkind. She needs something... purer."

Kado's eyes fell upon his mother, dying at the feet of her children. "I cannot," he said. "I can't kill my own mother."

"Nor can I," agreed Briaca.

"You won't have to," Oksana said sadly, "because you *cannot*. I already released my poison and tainted my blood for all who would drink of it. If you drank it now, it would destroy you like this same poison once killed Dominus Titus."

"Then how?" Kado asked, looking around. All the other dragonkind still watched, but seemed unwilling to make the sacrifice.

"I am Argant," the old man quietly explained, "called the Ancient One. The form you see is not my own, but of my vinculum, Erwan the Bold. He granted me this body so that I may once again walk among the humankind. I am a dragon walker, able to appear as human while still clinging to my elder form." The skeletal dragon shook, rattling bones and giving off a bit of flame from its nostrils.

"So you really are the original Lord of Fire?" Briaca asked, her voice filled with awe.

"Yes. I am the same."

"I saw that," Kado realized, "just a few minutes ago while Lars and Briaca..." he could not finish the sentence, refusing to put into words what his sister had done.

"Yes," Argant agreed. "Goro's memories flow through you just as they did your sister. But you will also receive mine if you choose our form. Erwan did not bond an aerouant as in the stories I have passed down to cover the truth, nor did he bond a mere Elderkin. He boldly bonded the sire of all dragonkind then gave up his life so that the Lord of Fire would walk among men."

"Why?" the boy demanded. "Why would anyone make such a sacrifice?"

"Ask your mother," the old man said.

Kado opened his mouth to ask, but Briaca spoke instead. "Why, Mother?" she asked. "Why did you sacrifice yourself for us?"

"My mission among humans was to provide the conduits for this new form of dragonkind. Just as Argant is a dragon walker through

Erwan's sacrifice, so may both of you gain dragon form through another's sacrifice. Once you have been redeemed you will change. That you have been tainted by the vampure will grant resistance to the disease that lives in vampure saliva. You will be cured, you will transform, and you will walk this earth with longevity, strength, and the wisdom of your ancestors."

"But you will still be dead," Kado protested, "and so will Father."

"You would have outlived us both nonetheless," Oksana said dismissively. Her strength had faded to the point she could barely talk. "I'm tired now and need to sleep. Make your choice, but remember you will have consequences either way you decide."

"I want redemption," Briaca said immediately. She did not need time to decide.

Kado wanted to reply just as quickly, but something bothered him deeply. Mother had sacrificed her life for her children, had allowed those vampure to drain her until Argant and his thunder could arrive. She now lay before him dying.

"Who?" the boy asked. "Mother's bond will transform me as her vinculum, but who else must give up their life so that Briaca may become one of these..." *Dragon walkers*, he said the word in his mind. It sounded foreign, even there. "Will it be Dregal? Because he doesn't seem to care for us at all!"

Argant met the boy's defiance with a somber smile. "You knew me as the storyteller, and so I shall tell you a tale. I shall speak to you of Argant the Ancient, the sire of dragonkind."

Chapter Twelve

Argant told his story without the aid of magic, lit by the moon high above and accompanied by the soft crackling of a dying fire. There was no need for theatrics, the graveness of the situation had built enough tension and expectation in everyone. The mood was set, and all eyes and ears focused on his tale.

"Goro," Argant repeated, "his name as ancient as mine. He, like I, was among the first Keryx conceived. Before us there were only two races, those heavenly beings sent to watch over mankind and the humans themselves. But species do not stay separated long, and soon their offspring became the substance of legends."

"The Romans called you Titans." Kado whispered, "Mother taught me that." He looked in Oksana's direction. So much of her strength had failed. He yearned to rush to her side, but his hands and feet remained bound by Argant's magic.

"Yes, and so did the Hellenes. The people of Judea call us Nephilim, and the Aryans had their own names. All of mankind remember the echoes of our existence, even if they have begun to forget our offspring."

Briaca looked to Kado and he nodded. They had both seen and experienced this part of the story. "You defeated Goro," she explained. "He fled the battlefield and hid underground but reemerged something... *worse* than the vampure. Why *did* you turn on him? How did you know he couldn't be trusted?"

"I realized too late the plans of Goro, how he had instigated our cousins to start the Ancient War. *He* created that division, the distrust, the fear. Once we were at odds, we did the work for him, warring until weakened. After some had died and others had gone, disappearing into another realm, I called him out, though I could not prove what he had done. Thus we fought against each other. He fell upon me with his first legion, a mixture of voltur and vampure he had created in secret."

Telling this story saddened Argant, the painful memories difficult to tell. This was a legend few had ever heard, no human, certainly, and, by their expressions, only very few dragonkind.

"I thought I had defeated him, but I never found his body. While I reveled in the victor's celebration he, as you both have seen, descended into darkness to wait. While I took on a form of abundance and plenty, Goro transformed into one of eternal thirst and wanton damnation."

"You had no idea he was amassing another army?" Kado asked.

"His legions walked among the humans we looked down upon but never actually saw. It wasn't until I noticed our kind had dwindled over many eons, first losing friends, then family, and finally offspring," Argant lamented, "that I realized Goro was to blame."

"You had no warriors among you at that time?" Briaca inquired.

"No, mostly wyvern and drake. I was the only one wearing the form we now call Elderkin, which, as you see, is quite limited in movement. We took our time and developed the aerouant form, agile warriors who could best strike the vampure from the sky as well as endure most of their damage. I fought alongside these warriors, already battle-hardened and scarred myself, but my presence put our kind at significant risk if I were to fall. We nearly lost that second war as soon as it began, not anticipating Goro's warfare would include ambush and surprise. We lost so many scales and regrew just as many, yet we persevered. Eventually, we triumphed, earning a lasting peace for centuries and more."

Listening to Argant's tales, the boy measured the weariness lining the old man's voice. He was tired of many things, the greatest of which, it seemed, was living.

"After the second war I settled down, took many spouses, and did my part to replenish our number. I allowed the greatest of our warriors to adopt the Elderkin form, the remains of which are those among us tonight."

He gestured weakly to the skeletal dragon now sleeping soundly beside Oksana. "What remains of me will soon be gone. I had no conception of time, nor how many more eon I would live. I had grown soft, my actions complacent, enjoying the lifestyle my children and grandchildren enjoyed. We were the apex predator, stewards of the earth responsibly harvesting its bounty at will. Very few took on the aerouant form. There was no need for protectors. But one day all that changed."

Briaca, having lived out the actions of Goro in her mind, knew what he was about to say. She knew the Lord of Blood very well. Too well for her liking.

"But soon we noticed subtle signs that danger had returned to the world. Hunters failed to return home to the thunder and children disappeared while playing in the fields. These were dismissed as accidents or disregarded as chance. We could not conceive of the evil that had returned."

"Goro," Briaca whispered sadly.

Argant visibly shuddered, deeply disturbed by the name. "Goro," he agreed solemnly.

"He's awful," she said, her hands trembling as they rubbed her arms against a chill. "The sensation I felt when he spoke... It was overbearing," she explained, "forcing me to relax and give myself over to Lars. He took me to a place in my mind and showed me stories, much like these you tell."

"And now he is coming again," Kado warned. "The voltur said so."

"Yes. He awakened during the time of Erwan the Bold. I sought him then, but he was hidden too well."

From high above, the sound of frantic flapping mixed with grunts of pain. All eyes looked upward to find Dregal, the large aerouant, had returned. His snakelike body reflected the moonlight, but several darker areas revealed scales had been ripped away by attackers. Some parts of his fleshy skin even bled.

"Did you find Lars?" Argant demanded.

"Lars fled eastward toward Dacia. I followed but was met by a horde of vampure. They swarmed me as I flew and, by the time I had fought enough of them off, I could no longer find Lars' scent. The sun is rising soon, so they allowed me to turn back. The Delta has disappeared and seeks his master."

"Goro," Argant again whispered quietly. "Lars will be elevated in his new form and will serve his dark master directly. With Lord Eduard's death, another will be chosen to fill his vacancy, and so on. If there are as many under the Evil One's command as you say, then our enemy has indeed grown strong enough to leave their shadows. We are weak and cannot fight a war, and so we must again go into hiding. We must hide away and transform our species one more time."

As if overwhelmed by the news, Oksana let out a final breath and died. Briaca watched as something changed in that exact moment within her brother. Through what she assumed was his bond to Mother, his body received part of her in the passing. His body quivered as if chilled and his eyes grew wide. All eyes turned toward the dragon's lifeless husk, then focused on Kado and Briaca.

"What do you choose, Briaca, daughter of Oksana?" Argant challenged. "Will you give in to the disease, joining forces with Goro, or choose to cleanse it through the blood of our kind?"

Tears filled her eyes just as remorse consumed her heart. "I want redemption," she said without hesitating. Argant's invisible force released her body at once, and she ran first to her father, dragging his body next to his wife. Kneeling beside the hot embers, she hugged them both and sobbed, quietly begging their forgiveness.

"And you, Kado the Courageous? Now that your mother's power has passed into you?"

"I choose transformation, to become a dragon walker and protector of our kind." Argant's magic dissipated and the boy ran to Briaca's side. He knelt, wrapping her shoulders with the soothing forgiveness she sought. Looking up at the storyteller he pleaded, "But please tell me who must make the sacrifice Briaca needs."

Yes, she wondered, *what sacrifice in the world could wash away my sins against Father and brother? What could purge my mind of the love I nearly felt for Lars?*

"To cleanse the vampure disease you must both consume pure dragon sanguis, the rarest and most ancient of all. For either of you to transform into what we need, you must consume what remains of *me.*"

Kado nodded. He had already assumed as much.

"I will do it," Briaca said quietly, though the thought of ever consuming more sanguis sickened her soul.

"I will too," her brother promised.

And thus Kado the Courageous and Briaca the Brave agreed to consume both Argant the Ancient and Erwan the Bold, joining the greatest legends in the history of dragonkind.

Chapter Thirteen

The dragons helped convey Kado and Briaca far away from Goro's reach, flying them to a primitive, mostly uninhabited continent. Though mountains here were high, they were not near the grand, unscalable peaks the Romans had named the *Alpes*. A more suitable place was found, a deep cavern of strong granite with only bats to witness their metamorphosis.

Argant dismounted the skeletal remains of his former self, leading the children and his entire thunder underground. They would sleep for nearly two thousand years, perhaps a bit longer depending upon whatever bit of Oksana had been passed to the boy. Yes, Kado would be special, but how much so depended on their bond and how much his mother had given of herself before passing. That vinculum would strengthen the boy's senses but wouldn't fully emerge until long after eclosion.

"Here is suitable," the Ancient One said to all assembled. Turning to Dregal he added, "Guard the entrance to this cavern with your life, and do so until both have awakened. Our future depends upon their form."

The mighty aerouant nodded his agreement, making no argument against.

To Briaca and Kado, Argant said, "Your mother was not the only of my children to sire my lineage on this earth. After I took human form, and for nearly four hundred years, I spread my seed across the Roman Empire so that you will have allies in the future."

"How will we find them, your offspring?" Briaca asked.

"I will still be with you, rather my memories will remain. But your slumber will be a long one and the awakening will not be pleasant.

You will emerge from your chrysalis confused, blind, and afraid, but those feelings will pass. Eventually, that amnesia will fade, and you will share all the knowledge I have amassed over three hundred million years, dating to the arrival of our heavenly ancestors."

"How will we survive two thousand years" Kado wondered aloud, "without eating or drinking?"

"How does a caterpillar survive in its cocoon during metamorphosis? It has devoured so many nutrients by the time it forms the chrysalis, the larva needs no more. Its heart slows as the body changes, growing new tissues and organs for the new form. So too will yours."

Argant watched Briaca carefully. Her control over the vampure urges had already waned during their journey. If she were to avoid transforming into vampure, she would need to purge their poison with pure sanguis very soon. "There's no point dragging this out any further," he said. "The time for my death has arrived."

"How much of you will we need to drink?" Kado asked quietly, repulsed by the thought.

Briaca, on the other hand, seemed eager—too eager.

"You must drink until *all* of me is gone."

Kado touched his mouth, touching freshly emerged fangs. He appeared worried over much more than just the feeding, and stole a glance at his sister.

Argant read the worry in her eyes. She feared she would choose the wrong form upon awakening, and knew Kado believed she might.

Briaca's eyes had finished their transformation and already reflected the blood of her thirst. Argant pitied her, but pain and confusion would prove necessary. Had Erwan not slain his own children, they would have been the first hybrids instead of these. But he had, and it took the Ancient One four hundred years to prepare again for this moment. But these were stronger versions than he originally planned, Erwan's obstinance had done him a favor after all.

Argant held out his wrists for the children. Their thirst needed no urging. The thunder looked away, repulsed by the sight, but the skeletal remains of the Ancient One curled around the trio as they feasted. The Lord of Fire watched with pride as his grandchildren consumed his sanguis, freely given and without poison. Only after his eyes became too weak to remain open did he allow them to close.

Chapter Fourteen

Caves Near Austin, Tx, Two Years Ago

"Briaca!" the man named Vince gently shook her arms. "Stay with me," he still spoke to her in Gaulish, which helped ground her mind more quickly.

She opened her eyes, focusing on his face. There was something about this man she trusted. He was friendly, fatherly even, and very pleasant. But, at the same time, there lurked something else she hated. She couldn't quite put her finger on that but thought it had something to do with her new memories.

She had not felt this way before.

Those remembrances of home—of Lars and Kado, and of Mother being a dragon, they had all rushed into her mind. So too did those of Father and what awful thing she had done. But so also were the things she had learned from Goro and Titus, even those from Lars. Now she also knew more from Argant the Ancient. Briaca was a sum of all these experiences but, most of all, she finally knew who and what she was.

I am a hybrid, of equal parts dragon and vampure.

She looked around, taking in the camp. These people had been so friendly, even if their Germanic language had sounded odd. Seeing again their strange clothing and technology, now that she remembered where she was and why, meant she had truly been asleep nearly two thousand years.

Things turned out just as Argant had promised.

Vince had grown worried by her sudden silence. With a low voice he encouraged, "Talk to me, Briaca." She wanted to, could tell he was a good man, despite something still felt off.

"I'm here," she responded in Gaulish. "I feel better."

"Good," he smiled. "I thought I lost you." He said *I*, not *we*, even odder. "Now, before you wig out on me again, I think we were talking about where you are from. You said *Cardac*, but I don't know this place. Where is Cardac, Briaca. Is it close by?"

"No." She shook her head, trying to remember what the Romans had called her land. Their word had always seemed so arrogant to her, that her people were so meaningless these invaders had changed the name of the conquered. Then she remembered, "Helvetia."

"Helvetia," the man repeated. "That sounds familiar, but I can't place it. What's it near?"

"Montes," she said.

"Which mountains?"

Again, she needed the Roman word. "Alpes."

Vince lit up. "Alps! You're from Switzerland! You are from Helvetia near the Alpes mountains?"

Briaca nodded, offering a soft smile.

One of the girls stared at her flat, glowing device, and asked in their odd language, "Isn't Helvetia the ancient *Roman* name for Switzerland, professor?" Briaca wished she could understand their exchange.

He frowned. "It is, and that's what worries me. No one's called it that since 1848. Either this gal's lost her marbles, or she's not from our time."

The other girl stepped closer, the young men stood by the vehicle, keeping watch but playing it off like they were merely visiting quietly on their own. "You mean time travel, Dr. Redder?"

Time, tima, more Germanic. Briaca assumed they discussed the time of day.

"No, I mean I think she's what we came here to find, and I'm getting really uncomfortable around her."

"I know," one of the young women agreed. "Have you been watching her eyes? They keep turning blood red."

Eye... Ay-eh, more Germanic. *Red...* pronounced *read,* it meant *ruber,* like the crimson color. Briaca realized both girls and Vince were looking directly at her eyes.

Something was wrong. Panic tried to take over but she forced it down. These people knew what she really was. If not, they would figure it out very soon.

Briaca took a closer look at the camp and the items each of the people carried. The men by the vehicle each wore a sheathed blade at their side, too short to be a sword but two broad to be a knife. She had never seen this style, but imagined it would do the same sort of damage as the former. All three also had a different type of sheath, one that held a black, metal device with a short handle to grip in their dominant hand. She realized this too must be some kind of weapon, and each of the girls wore one on their hip as well.

Now that she knew what to look for, she realized Vince carried one of each, both a blade and one of these other devices. These were soldiers, and they knew what she was. Briaca tried to get up slowly, to make it easier to get away.

"Relax," Vince urged her in Gaulish, motioning for her to remain seated. To the others he said, "We've spooked her somehow."

Not time of day, they knew she was not from this time period. "When?" Briaca demanded. "When is now?"

"I don't understand. *When?*"

"*Tima,* time. When is now?"

Vince said nothing as he considered her question.

"Professor," the first young woman said, "I think you're right, she means what year."

"Why would she ask that?" the second asked. "How does she know?"

"Because," the teacher said with a sigh, "she's a Gaulish woman from Switzerland, calling herself a resident of a village named Cardac. The closest etymology of the name would be Cardaci, the Roman term used for wool traders and sheep herders. The village doesn't exist today, because it was named for a region, that which the Romans attributed to that industry they found among the Alps when they arrived."

"I don't understand," the young woman admitted.

"This girl," the professor explained, "who stumbled out of a cave with blood red eyes and no clothes, speaking a mixture of Latin, Gaulish, and Germanic, is not from around here. She came to us from a far corner of Gaul, one barely ever controlled by the Roman Empire because it was too mountainous for their legions. Daphne, this woman is over two thousand years old."

"Legion! *Legionis*!" Briaca repeated. Her eyes grew wider, full of fear upon recognizing that one word while the man spoke his native language.

"Yes, *legion*. What about a legion, Briaca? Why does that word trouble you? Do you remember the Roman legions? Did they harm you? Is that who made you a vampire?"

"Vampire?" The word made no sense to Briaca, but she understood his general meaning. After first noticing her eyes, he was asking which legion of vampure she belonged to. Of course, there was no word for vampure in either Gaulish or Latin, so he had used the closest word to the Greek. "*Ego sum vyrkolakas*," she admitted sadly, then burst into tears.

"What did she say?" Daphne insisted.

Vince opened his mouth to answer but a loud crash interrupted whatever he meant to say. A horn honked and a whining siren broke the stillness of the night. Both young men lay on the ground, dazed after being slammed hard into their vehicle.

Standing over the bodies of both young men was a Gamma vampure.

"Hello, Briaca," Lars said with a smile.

Vince never took his eyes off the creature when he stood and asked, "Is this a *friend* of yours, Briaca? An old boyfriend, perhaps? You just said, *ego sum vyrkolakas*. Around here, we call them vampires."

"No," she answered truthfully. She wanted nothing to do with her former Salvator. "But I do know him."

Speaking flawlessly in that odd, Germanic mixture, Lars addressed Vince. "The word *vampire* is such an insult, hunter. It means *witch* in Hungary, but we are *so* much more than that."

Vince motioned for the girls to get behind him, inching his way toward the back of the vehicle. "Is she one of yours, then? She got away and you're rounding her up?"

Without looking at Briaca, Vince reached down and offered a hand. She took it and pulled herself up to stand, looking around for any weapon she could find.

Lars never took his eyes off his Sigma. "I've waited so long for you, Briaca. I couldn't feel you until tonight. Whatever Argant did, he silenced your mind from me. But I knew it was you the moment you awakened." He reached out his hand. "Come away with me, it can be as it should have been."

"No." She moved behind Vince with the other girls. The man's hands rested one each on his weapons, hesitating, ready to draw them but not wishing to startle Lars.

"Step aside, hunter, so I may claim what's mine."

"I clearly heard her say *no*, and in Texas that's a clear denial of consent. So, go on. I think it's time you fly on out of here." Vince made a shooing motion with his hands as he spoke. The moment he did, Briaca rushed forward, drawing Vince's short blade and lunging at Lars.

All at once Vince and the girls drew their strangely shaped weapons, pointing them at Lars. "Don't shoot!" Vince cautioned. "Not till she's out of the way!"

"But she's one of him!" Daphne protested.

"I'm not so sure."

Briaca dipped low as Lars swung massive arms to grab her, ducking nearly twice as fast as the vampure could move. Time seemed to stand still as she slid on one knee, moving behind him as she raised back to full height. She noticed the blade was black instead of shiny, some kind of iron, she guessed, and slid it across Lars' side to test its effect.

The cut sizzled, steamed, belching gasses as it dragged, causing the vampure to cry out with pain. His eyes changed, boiling darker red with anger as he spun around to face his former Sigma. She plunged the blade deep, her quickness catching him by surprise. He moved as if underwater, sluggishly trying to catch the blade as it drove into his bowels.

"Duck!" Vince shouted.

Briaca knew he meant to use his weapons, and rolled out of the way to the other side of the vehicle. Loud explosions rang out in the night, and the smell of smoke and sulfur reached her nose. As she peeked around a black wheel, she watched several inches of flame explode from the muzzles of the weapons.

Dark circles immediately popped up on Lars' body. A streak of skin ripped away from his cheek, breaking off one of the bony ridges below his left eye. That's when Briaca realized these weren't circles but holes. Whatever their weapons were, Vince and the girls used them again and again until each fell silent. Vince pushed a button on the side of his and a piece of metal fell to the ground. Pulling another from his waistband, he shoved it beneath the weapon and the top of it slammed shut.

Lars staggered angrily, his wounds smoking and steaming as if the weapon had thrown fire, then ran toward the professor. Several more explosions rang out, taking him squarely in the chest and driving him backward. With an angry scream he leaped, his broad wings pushing the air downward as he rose into the sky, up and over Vincent's head. He flew east, disappearing into high clouds.

Briaca stood, walking slowly around the vehicle, wondering if the weapons would fire at *her* next. She placed her hands in front of her, dropping the knife now dripping with steaming blood.

She stared at Vince in the moonlight, watching him closely and noticing his eyes had changed. They now glowed like fiery orbs. She stepped closer with empty hands, ignoring the weapons trained on her by the girls.

"Not vampire," she said in her best imitation of that odd blend of Germanic. Stepped closer to the professor. She saw it, now, the reason this man both pleased and offended her. Gone were Vince's human qualities. His eyes held the slightest bit of fire behind two dark irises. His skin, though outwardly human, was comprised of tiny scales interwoven and sprouting hair as if he were a mammal instead of reptilian. In his chest, a heart beat warm blood. "I... I am dragon, like you."

He said nothing, just stared into her eyes as Daphne stepped up behind her.

Something sharp pricked Briaca's neck like she had been stung by a wasp. She brought her hand away, finding just a bit of blood on her fingertip. Wooziness turned into blackness as she crashed, unconscious, into a heap on the ground.

Chapter Fifteen

Briaca awoke to city noise. At first it was soothing, letting her know she was not alone, that people walked the streets during daylight unafraid and unbothered by demons like Lars and Dominus Titus. Then a horn honked and people shouted.

Her eyes shot open, thinking Lars had returned. She remembered the young men, laying on the ground beside the strange vehicle, with the offensive noise the thing had made after they were slammed into its side.

She sat up, looking around at the tiny room. It had happened again. She was taken captive and locked away to transform. Only the door to this room stood open. She eyed it curiously.

Even more curious about the sounds outside, Briaca pushed aside luxurious bedding, soft and warm. She had never seen any so clean. Rising, she moved to an open window left ajar to usher in the sounds below.

Dozens of those strange vehicles moved beneath her, a dizzying distance below. She never imagined buildings could reach so high. Even in Aventicum they only ever reached two stories. She counted twenty on the building across the street. A light on the corner turned green, lighting up the symbol of a little man, and a dozen people crossed at once while all the vehicles stopped and waited.

"It's obnoxious, isn't it?" Vince asked in Gaulish from the doorway.

Briaca turned. The man held a mug of hot liquid in his right hand, his body leaning against the entrance. He wore an odd tunic of a winking, smiling man with an outstretched thumb and pointed forefinger. The image resembled the Christian martyr-god, wearing Judeo-Roman robes and a red heart on his chest.

"What's obnoxious?" she asked, even though she had not understood the word.

"The city. It's called *Austin*. It's supposed to represent progress but, when I look down, you know what I see? People in a hurry to get nowhere. They're so intent on *getting* to that nowhere, they don't even notice each other until one of them gets in their way. Then its yelling, honking, and a flurry of hand gestures. When they finally get to their nowhere, they just sit there, miserable, until it's time to hurry home and do the same thing the next day. Like I said, obnoxious."

She looked down at the people in a rush, just as he described. "I like it," she said. "To me they're not going *nowhere*. They're doing *something* by going *somewhere*. I think it's a good thing not to be cooped up all day, tending a home that's always too cold or too dirty or cooking a meal for your ungrateful family who only notice when there isn't one." She shook her head, "I'd rather have *this*, than a prison." She turned, confronting the professor with angry eyes. "Am I in another prison?"

Vince stepped aside from the door, gesturing down the hall. "You're free to come this way, with me, to answer all the questions I have. Or," he pointed at the open window, "leave and climb down the fire escape." He shrugged. "You're free, but I'd really like answers." Without waiting for a response he turned, moving down the hall.

Briaca stood for a moment, watching the people and vehicles scurrying below, and decided to follow the professor. She found him sitting in a dining room in front of a black, flat box. The part facing him showed colorful images.

In the adjoining room, one of the young men and the woman named Daphne sat curled on a sofa, watching another flat box with moving pictures of talking people. These entranced her. Though she could not understand their language, the people trapped in the box seemed happy, joking and laughing as they interacted. This made Daphne and her male friend laugh as well, and that made Briaca smile. She had not done so for quite some time.

"It's called a television," Vince explained without looking up. He pointed at what appeared to be a kitchen nearby, unused and, by the look of it, *never* used. A white bag with an orange *W* rested on the counter. "Have some breakfast and some joe, if you want."

"Joe?" she asked.

"It's a drink that wakes you up. Grab a mug but be careful, the pot is hot."

Briaca wasn't thirsty, but curiosity and a growling belly sent her peeking into the bag. It was full of smaller pieces of yellow parchment, each wrapped around some kind of food. She pulled one out, ripped off the paper, and frowned at the white casing. Tearing it open, she recognized eggs and sausage. She sat down beside the professor and devoured three.

Vince took a sip from his mug. "They're good, aren't they."

She nodded, mouth too full to answer.

"Here in Texas we get along about most everything, but there's still a few details we fight over. The first being whether to call these things breakfast tacos or burritos." He shrugged. "I guess it depends on how you vote."

She had no idea what he was talking about, but nodded along as she ate.

Vince finally took a good look at the girl. He smiled warily, but his eyes expressed frustration.

"What is wrong?" she asked.

"You," he said truthfully. "Everything about *you* is wrong." He pointed at strange letters and numbers on the box in front of him and explained. "After Daphne sedated you last night..."

"Sorry about that, by the way!" the girl waved a hand without turning to look away from the television when she apologized.

Vince continued. "I sent a bit of your blood to a friend of mine at the University Biology Lab. Wanted him to take a look at it. The results are unlike any I ever expected. I've only seen these twice before."

"I don't understand. What would someone learn by looking at blood?"

He frowned, finding it difficult to express these details in Gaulish. "I tested you, have the results, and still don't understand a thing about you. You're the first person I've ever met with DNA markers like mine. I thought I was a mutant for decades until I learned what I was, and here you are, walking out of a cave as my distant cousin."

"We're dragonkind," Briaca explained.

He flinched at the word but continued. "But you're also something else. I've been hunting vamps for twenty years, but you're the first I've seen that's also..." he couldn't say *dragon*, and so he finished with, "like me."

"What will you do with me?" she asked.

"I don't know, but I don't think you're a threat. Your boyfriend made that apparent last night. But he wasn't happy when he left, so I'm worried he'll find you again. I don't think he'll stop until he has control over you."

"Lars," Briaca said the name aloud, the breakfast tacos no longer appetizing. "His name is Lars, and he was the vampure who tried to turn me."

"Tried? As in, wasn't successful? Or *did* turn you, but now you're in control of the virus?"

"Virus?"

"A sickness. That's all I ever thought vampirism was, just a virus like the flu. A stomach bug. Vamps to me were simply people who were incurably ill, except those like Lars. He's the real deal, as his blood sample on my knife also proved. His DNA is altered, reconfigured into a different species of human—like ours but much different."

Briaca understood none of what he said but decided the gist was that he accepted her for being like him, despite her *other* properties. She wondered how much she could tell this man, how much of her story he could accept. She decided to tell him everything, beginning with Mother and ending with Argant. To Vince's credit he never flinched, never interrupted, and held his comments till the end.

"So it's true," he finally said.

"What is?"

He pointed to a Christian crucifix on the wall. "I was a priest. Went to college in Dallas Catholic Seminary, but did my graduate studies in Rome as soon as I was ordained. Until then I thought I was like everyone else, a bit different, sure, but human all the same. But I was put into a special program by the Vatican, investigating miracles at first, but later was brought into something darker. My job was to investigate the presence of vampires and *other* genetic irregularities. An old monsignor finally explained it was because they knew what I was, even if I didn't, and that they barely tolerated me as much more than a vamp. After a while, sick of brushing elbows with evil, I left the priesthood to hunt them."

"That's what you were doing last night?" Briaca asked. "You were hunting and found me?"

"I found more than just you." He turned the black box on the table so she could see the screen. With a tap and click, an image appeared.

Briaca gasped, seeing the cavern illuminated for the first time.

Vince tapped a finger on a broken egg. "This is yours, isn't it? What you crawled out of right before Daphne, Paul, Jake, and Lois found you?"

Briaca had decided she would not keep any secrets from this man and was now relieved she had told him the truth. He had seen and now knew it all.

He placed a finger on the large dragon skull resting quietly in the image. "This is Argant?"

She nodded.

"And this," he tapped the unhatched egg, "is your brother? This is Kado?"

Tears welled up unexpectedly, and Briaca buried her eyes. She wished so badly for her brother to be here. The thought of him alone in that cave nearly broke her heart. *And I just left him there!* She noticed the satchel laying on the ground, the dragon's tooth laying where she had left it nearby.

"What's wrong?" Vince asked, reading the sudden change in her eyes.

"I… I just realized I left something very important behind."

"Hmm," Vince grunted reaching into a backpack sitting on the floor beside him. He drew out the dragon's tooth and another piece of bone, parts of Argant's foot by the looks of it. He set these on the table. He pointed at the tooth. "A summoning horn?" he asked.

"Also a weapon."

"I see. What makes it so effective? So far, only iron seems to affect those things."

"A dragon's bite is deadly to a vampure, and their teeth and bones make just as deadly weapons against them."

Vince thought again, swishing his big mustache around while he did. Finally, he reached into the bag and pulled out three small pieces of forged and brightly polished metal—brass by the looks of them, with a darker metal on each tip. "These are bullets," he said, then set one of the hand weapons on the table, one of those he had used the night before. "This is a gun. This fires those bullets very fast. Usually the tips are made of lead, but a friend of mine modified these out of an iron alloy. I thought they would work."

"I saw how they worked on Lars."

"Not very well," Vince admitted.

"No," Briaca agreed, "not very well."

Next he pulled out the short knife Briaca had taken from his belt the night before, that she had plunged into Lars. It was cleaned, the source of the samples Vince had tested. "This knife," he explained, "is forged from tempered iron. It worked well, better than the bullets, it seems."

"Dragon bone works better," Briaca insisted. She pointed at the tooth. "This cuts even better than a knife."

Vince considered this, sitting in silence while people inside the television chattered away. The music changed abruptly and the people faded. Soon another person appeared, seated at a table and speaking to the viewers. An image beside his head showed the smiling faces of a man and woman, waving as they stepped into a large vehicle.

Briaca stood, not believing her eyes, and approached the box on the wall.

"Turn that up," Vince demanded in his Germanic dialect, and Daphne tapped buttons on a small object beside her.

The announcer said, "President Morales and his wife visited Galveston this morning accessing the damage left by Hurricane Isaac."

A closer image of the diplomat appeared, as he spoke to a crowd. "All of our nation mourns with you, Texas, for the loss of life and property this proud state experienced this weekend. I assure you I'm doing everything I can to ensure aid arrives promptly and have declared this region a *state of emergency,* so FEMA can get started doing its job."

"What is this man's name?" Briaca demanded, wildly tapping the image of his face.

"Tito Morales," Vince replied. "He's our nation's leader."

"No." Briaca shook her head angrily. "It's Titus! *Dominus* Titus Aurelius! I can never forget his face!"

"What about him, Briaca?" Vince asked cautiously, something else not sitting right with him.

"He serves Goro! He's vampure!"

"Well then we have a bigger problem," the young man beside Daphne exclaimed, pointing at the screen.

"In other news," the announcer declared, "well-known Texas Democrat super donor and activist, Laurel Perkins, cancelled his own visit to Galveston, his spokesman citing health issues and an urgent need for bed rest. Perkins is best known for the campaign stomping he did for President Morales when he was governor of Texas during the election." The image of the smiling man, with his red hair but emerald eyes, hovered above the announcer. Everyone in the room recognized him.

"Lars," Briaca accused, abruptly punching his face and cracking the screen.

"So it would seem," Vince agreed. All eyes turned to him. "Well," he said, downing his cup of joe, "it seems we've got our work cut out for us." He pointed to the dragon bone on the table. "Paul, run that metatarsal specimen to our friends at the campus forge. Tell them I want five bowie knives as soon as possible."

Paul scooped them up, quickly making for the door.

"Paul!"

The young man froze, turning for more instructions.

"Take a bit to the Colonel too. Tell him the heads on these 9 mil were too heavy, sluggish and barely broke the skin on that vamp. If he can make something lighter, I'd be much obliged."

Paul snapped a fake salute. "Right away, Doc!"

Turning to Briaca, Vince explained. "A few hundred years after you went into your egg, a group of invaders came out of Denmark and Sweden. History called them *Vikings*. They were wicked smart for barbarians and found a way to strengthen their iron weapons by folding the heated metal with bone instead of charcoal. I want to test a theory out, using your old friend to see if he makes our iron weapons more potent. Let's see if he helps us."

At first she was startled, but quickly saw the reasoning. "Argant would have been happy to be used in such a way," she agreed.

"Great. Now tell me, are you up for adventure, Briaca? How would you like to see the campus?"

She pointed outside the window. "Among the people?"

Vince grinned behind his mustache. "Among a *lot* of people."

Briaca beamed, "Then yes!"

"Good. Daphne, find this girl some proper clothes, and teach her how to use a shower. She stinks like rotten eggs."

Chapter Sixteen

Briaca learned much crossing the streets to the campus, specifically that green means go, red means stop, and honking is for expressing your feelings when driving a vehicle. She knew these now as cars and trucks. The big ones, like Vince drove to the cave, she learned as SUVs, but his was special, a *classic* he called an '86 Bronco.

She also learned that which finger you use when communicating with other pedestrians was crucial. Vince had to step in and help her out on this one. It almost got them all into trouble.

She marveled at the pools, fountains, and especially the tall watchtower, finding the architecture unique but oddly familiar to that of the Romans. The *campus*, as Vince called it, turned out a city within a city, just as bustling but with younger faces. It was a place for learning. He led her to one of the older buildings, calling it *Ben Hall*. His office, he said, was in the basement.

"I like it down there," he added. "I don't get bothered as much."

She and Daphne followed the professor down a flight of stairs away from the main building. Vince cringed when a voice called out from an open door.

"Doctor Redder!" a man demanded his time. "Step in *here*, please."

Daphne explained as the mustached man stepped inside and shut the door behind him, "That's Devin Fields, the Academic Dean. He's Vince's boss." Raised voices told Briaca all she needed to know—these men were not friends. Vince came storming out after only a few minutes, red in the face and a bit shaken. "What is it?" Daphne asked her professor.

"Funding increased for both linguistics *and* European Studies, but mine is cut off completely. Apparently they can't *account* for all my project money."

Reading Briaca's confusion, he explained the problem to her in Gaulish. "Without funding we have no operation—no tracking or hunting of vamps. I get some of what we need through friends and favors, but this is expensive business."

"Is it over?" asked Daphne.

"Not by a longshot." He pushed opened the door to his office. "Welcome to the Dragon Lair," he said with a wink.

The office itself was a desk in the corner of the room. One of those flat televisions was mounted on the wall beside it, with two more, smaller screens on the tabletop. Vince explained these were *monitors* for him to plug in his box. That was a *laptop.* He said it was like having a library and an entire team of thousands of scribes working inside the little box, doing computations and retrieving information in seconds.

The rest of the room stood empty except for some metal lockers and storage cabinets, some wrestling mats, and some hanging bags. The cabinets he kept locked, grumbling that someone had tried to get into one recently. Probably Dean Fields. "Nosey little bastard," the professor grumbled as he popped it open. "Over here, Briaca," he beckoned. "This is what I wanted to show you."

Inside were dozens of artifacts dedicated to vampire hunting. He pulled out a device meant to be worn, a high collar fashioned from dragon scales. She had seen this before. "Erwan the Bold wore that when he fought against Dominus Titus."

"I thought you might recognize it. A friend of mine found it in a cave in the Alps. From what I can tell, it was worn by some of the earliest vampire hunters about the time the Romans arrived."

Briaca watched Vince place it back in the case, then pause to run his fingers across another artifact. This was a crucifix. He appeared sad while briefly touching it, perhaps missing that part of his life. He quickly shrugged off the feeling.

"This is what got me into hunting," he explained, pulling out a human skull. As he turned it around, Briaca recognized two long fangs. "I was still in the Jesuit Order then, when I was sent to investigate an archeological site. My buddy Severus Blanc uncovered bones and iron trinkets from a shallow grave, and also that collar. But carbon dating was inconclusive. We later realized the body was buried first, then someone dug it up and later added the collar to the grave."

"That had to have been by a loved one," Briaca realized, someone who knew where she was buried."

"Exactly, which told me she wasn't a vamp when she was buried, but a victim to one."

"Adelia," Briaca exclaimed, "was Erwan's wife! Titus said she couldn't raise because Erwan tainted her grave."

Vince nodded agreement. "That's what I concluded, based on the legends and what you told me this morning." The sadness had returned. "But I didn't stop there. I had to know more, so I kept this skull. I took a sample and brought it to a friend of mine here at the college. He called me later and wanted to know if this was a hoax. He said one of the people who handled her DNA was a close match. But that couldn't have been Severus—he was always careful. This woman turned out a distant cousin to me, but she *wasn't* human. He didn't know *what* she was. He gave me the sequence, and I looked it up in the Vatican's forensic database."

"She was a dragon, and you realized you were too."

"Exactly." Vince carefully returned the skull to its spot on the shelf and closed and locked the cabinet. "That's when I left the priesthood and started hunting vamps."

"But you've never seen a real dragon, nor another person like you?"

"Not until I met you last night."

"It's ready!" Daphne interrupted, turning on the television. After a few clicks on the laptop, an image appeared of a huge manor.

"Wow, that's one helluva mansion," Vince exclaimed.

"It's called *Villa Del Lago*," Daphne explained, "and it's not far away. Only twenty or thirty minutes."

"Who lives there?" Briaca asked.

"That belongs to your boyfriend, Lars, or should I say, *Laurel Perkins.* He's one of the wealthiest men in Texas, but no one really knows where he gets his money. A lot of it comes from the big donors, and he just funnels it into Texas politics—always progressive projects."

Briaca understood. "That's what he told me Goro does. He buys influence and then makes things happen behind the scenes. He said the vampure control human society from the shadows, steering things so we never control our own lives."

Vince exchanged a look with Daphne. "That's pretty much what we've figured out, as well. But I had no idea it was this big. Not all the way to the President."

"How do we get inside?" Briaca asked, walking closer to look at the image on the screen. "He won't be alone."

"Good question," Daphne agreed, scribbling on a pad with a stylus. The words *Frontal Assault or B&E?* appeared on the monitor above the house.

The manor was lakeside, nestled in cliffs, and sat on twenty-five acres. Other homes, mansions as Vince called them, overlooked this one and would certainly call in soldiers or guards—police are what Daphne mentioned when Briaca was practicing using her middle finger.

Vince carefully approached Briaca, gently touching her shoulder and turning her to look at him. "*You* aren't getting inside," he said, pointing back and forth between him and Daphne. "She and I will, and so will Paul, Jake, and Lois. That's what *we* do."

"I'm stronger," she argued, "and faster."

"But you aren't trained. You don't know how to fight. I saw you last night. You only stabbed him because he was surprised and didn't expect you to be so fast."

"Who got stabbed?" A redheaded man with a wavy beard stood in the doorway.

"No one, Devin," Vince snapped, moving to push him out the door into the hall.

"Do *not* push me out!" the man said with authority. "I'm the Dean and this is my building. What in the hell is going on?" He looked up at the television screen, eyes growing wide. He recognized the home of the biggest political donor in Texas and read the words. "Frontal assault or breaking and entering? What kind of criminal activity are you teaching your graduate students? What does *any* of this have to do with languages or World Religions?"

"Devin," Vince pleaded, "it's not what it looks like."

At that exact moment Paul returned with a shorter man dressed in black tactical pants and a white polo shirt. He wore a gun on his hip, exposed for the world to see.

Dean Fields frowned at the weapon.

"I got your order!" the man declared, excitement booming in his voice. He noticed the manor on the screen. "Frontal assault? Out of the question, but we *could* make it appear like one. That'll get you inside. The vampire will be in the safe room, secure in the center of the mansion. It has separate ventilation and steel walls, so getting in there will be tough. I can get you the code, though. He'll be sleeping, if what Paul told me was accurate and those iron bullets beat him up so badly."

"Colonel," Vince said, pointing at the dean, "please stop."

"I can't believe iron bullets didn't work! I mean, they worked, obviously, but not like I'd hoped. This new formula should do the trick. Dragon bone makes sense, but no more 9mil. I've got a better idea!"

"Colonel!" Daphne shouted, pointing with both hands at the redheaded man about to turn and run to the police.

"Shotguns, that's what we need, we..." the Colonel paused, finally reading the room, and turned to face Devin. "Oh, hi. I didn't see you there." With a gruff hand he grabbed the man's shirt, just as the dean turned to run, and pulled him inside the basement, kicking the door shut with a slam. He led the terrified scholar to a chair and pushed him into it, using his hands to hold him down. "Guess I gotta deal with this guy, Vince?" he asked with a wink.

Vince groaned. "Devin, I'm sorry. You weren't supposed to ever know any of this."

The dean looked up at the bald professor and surprised everyone in the room. "I didn't believe it was true. When I found that skull I thought it was a fake. Are vampires real?"

Vince nodded. "They are."

"And you mentioned dragons. I saw that collar, the one made out of scales. I thought those were fake too."

"Nope. One hundred percent genuine. Dragons and vampires have fought this ancient war for eons, dating back to the first humans and…"

"I know. I teach medieval European history. I knew about the vampires, *always* thought they were real, but dragons? That's new," Devin explained. He pointed at *Villa del Lago*. "That's Laurel Perkin's house. I've met him. I've been in that house. He's *big* time. What's his role in all this?"

"He's a vampire," Paul said, rubbing his head absently where it had hit the Bronco the night before.

"Prove it," Devin demanded.

Vince shrugged and turned to Daphne. "Pull up the dash cam footage from last night. I was going to show it to the Colonel, anyways."

The girl nodded and tapped some keys. A box popped up on the monitor, a view from the Bronco. Jake and Paul leaned on the grill guard while Daphne, Lois, and Vince crouched in front of Briaca, speaking a mixture of Gaulish and Latin.

Devin looked at her as if just realizing this wasn't one of Vince's graduate students. "That's Gaulish, isn't it?" he asked in the language.

"It is," she answered back. "I'm from Helvetia."

The man simply nodded and turned his eyes to the monitor just as a large shape stepped into the frame, a creature easily eight feet tall with broad bone structure and ridges under his eyes and across his brow. A row of horns formed a perfect circle around his head. His wingspan was easily twenty feet wide. In the video, Jake and Paul looked up. The vampire easily smacked them into the side of the vehicle, setting off its car alarm.

Daphne paused it just as the creature's face turned into view.

"According to our new friend, Briaca, this vamp is named Lars. He poses in the real world as Laurel Perkins. He's pretty high up in the vampire hierarchy, I might point out."

"He's a Beta," Briaca suddenly realized. "He was only a Delta when I saw him last, and only freshly so."

Vince frowned and jumped in. "Apparently two thousand years is a long time, plenty to move up the chain. I knew there were different forms but not the names and descriptions of each. You know them all?" he asked Briaca.

She nodded.

"Good. Get with Daphne later, and get it all written down on paper. I want to know their strengths and weaknesses and compare what you know to what we've already figured out."

She promised she would.

Daphne hit a button and the video played.

Everyone watched as Briaca stabbed the knife in his belly, amazed at how fast she moved. She was literally a blur on the screen.

The Colonel frowned when the bullets struck Lars' body, then let go of Dean Fields. "How much more of that dragon bone have you got, Vince? I need to put together a lot of ball bearings."

"Ball bearings?" the professor asked.

"Buckshot," the Colonel said with a grin. "The 9mil was too big. It slowed down when it hit his body, just like it did in the ballistics gel when we tested it. Buckshot's smaller. It fans out and might tear a guy like him apart."

"Shrapnel," Paul suggested. "Make some of that too."

"Why?" Daphne asked.

Everyone turned at once, Vince, the Colonel, Paul, even Devin, replied together, "Grenades."

"Oh," The girl's eyes went wide.

Then Dean Fields surprised the room. "I want in. Whatever's going on, I want in!"

"I need my funding back," Vince said without hesitation. "I can't fight *shit* without money."

"Doubled… no, tripled! Whatever you need. I have private donors who will pitch in."

"The less who know about this the better, especially since the vamps fund programs all the time, trying to learn what people like us know about them."

"Frontal assault then. How soon can you get everything ready?" Vince asked the Colonel. "The plan of attack, new weaponry, all of it."

The shorter man looked deep in thought. "That depends on how much of that bone you've got."

Vince turned to Briaca, silently asking her approval, and she nodded. "We have plenty, but I need a rental truck, a large one with good shocks."

"Good," the Colonel said with a grin. "Get me as much bone as you can, and I'll have weapons to go tomorrow night. I think I can also try out some lighter sniper rounds, *if* we blend the bone with a mixture of lead and iron."

Vince pointed at Paul and Dean Fields. "You two go with him. Get blueprints of the property, the latest property description and layout, and compare it to what Devin remembers about the inside. I'll call Jake and have him get a couple of trucks. Daphne, you get Lois on the phone. Go rent some jet skis or a boat, something that involves bikinis and binoculars. Recon that entire cliffside and get an accurate head count of every person or vamp and where each of them are every hour. We've only got two days and one night to do this!"

Though he had spoken in what she now knew as English, Briaca had picked up on and followed most of what he said except a few words. But she had not heard her name mentioned at all.

"What about me, Vince?" she asked in her best attempt at their language.

"I already said you're not going." He pointed at the mostly empty room, gesturing at training dummies and heavy bags hanging in the corner. He pointed at the wrestling mats on the ground. "We train daily for this kind of thing and *know* how to fight. I don't want you to get killed."

She moved fast, a blur of movement that grabbed his arm and spun the professor around, flipping him over her shoulder the way her father once taught while wrestling with her and Kado. "I learn fast," she said into his ear as he lay on the ground.

"You'd better take her along, Vince," the Colonel suggested. "I've got someone who can teach her just enough to be helpful."

Vince nodded, rubbing his shoulder. "Make it so, Colonel."

Chapter Seventeen

Briaca scratched at the wide bite collar around her neck. The entire team was wearing them, meant to repel fangs. The cloth was itchy, but that's not what bothered her. It was so thin, despite being heavy, a material Vince had called *Kevlar*. She worried fangs would get through. They weren't tested on actual vampure, she had argued, pointing out the extra strength with which the creatures would bite. But everyone else seemed to trust the things.

She stayed close to the Colonel. Vince had assigned the two as *overwatch* while Jake and Lois comprised the strike team. Her job, as he explained, was to distract the guards with pyrotechnics and, if the need were to arise, heavier *things that go boom*, as he called them. The Colonel would guide Jake and Lois inside using a *radio*. That someone could whisper and still send their voice several furlongs was something Briaca still marveled at. Paul and Daphne were to hang out at the event pavilion, a holdover from when the previous owners of this property provided for weddings and parties.

Vince would provide a second overwatch from a higher altitude, overlooking the rear windows of the house while able to provide assistance should the team need back up or help getting out.

The plan was simple—make their way inside after or while drawing the guards outside. Since Lars was still likely injured, he would be sleeping it off in his panic room, sequestered from light which, as Briaca explained, interrupted the regeneration or transformation process. This was an assassination strike, a quick *get in and get out*, as Vince put it.

After the attack, either the second team or the Colonel would ready the boat, the one the girls rented to do reconnaissance, and escape to the far side of Lake Travis. They would have getaway cars waiting there. In the event they had to abort, or that they never made it to the other side, the Colonel said he had a way to *lift and hotwire a Tesla*, whatever that was, using the device he called a phone. Thankfully, nearly every neighbor in the estates had a Tesla, Daphne had reported.

One other thing they had in their favor was the night of this raid. It was a holiday, apparently, the fourth day of the month honoring Gaius Julius Caesar, the first Roman Emperor after ushering in the era of the Republic. According to the smiling faces of everyone else on the team, that date meant a thing called *fireworks*. Vince said Briaca would know what those were when she saw them.

"The fireworks display is estimated to last twenty minutes," Vince reminded the students as they set out for an afternoon of boating.

He dropped Briaca and the Colonel near the Episcopal church, careful to avoid neighborhood door cameras, and plenty early enough in the day that the panel van he had borrowed wouldn't seem out of place. It actually belonged to a student who cleaned pools for a thing called *beer money,* and who needed extra credit. Vince was dropped off later by Dean Fields who rode something called an Uber to meet up with his family to watch the fireworks display. The administrator would return home with them.

Everyone felt good about the plan, and each had memorized the terrain, their escape routes, and the layout of the house. Nothing would go wrong unless a guy named *Murphy* and his *law* showed up. At least that's what the Colonel had said.

By the time the sun set, everyone was in place and their communication earpieces worked fine. Briaca only wished this place called Texas wasn't so blasted hot.

Briaca lay on rocky ground, well-hidden on a ridge among cedar bushes. This was overwatch, far away from the action, and it felt boring. She wished she could talk to this man, called the Colonel, that he knew even the slightest bit of Latin, but had memorized hand signals in case of trouble or need to communicate.

He turned to her and held two fists together. *Are you ready?*

She moved her hand to touch her mouth. *Yes.*

The Colonel paused. He wasn't sure how to say what he wanted to next. He briefly rolled and acted like he fought an invisible enemy, kicking and punching the air, then turned to Briaca. Again two fists together. *Are you ready?*

She laughed. One of his friends was a fighting instructor, something called a *Marine,* and she had spent all morning with the man, learning to fight standing up as well as to grapple better on the ground. The emphasis was spent on keeping fangs from her neck. Given it was her first lesson, she thought she had done quite well. Her fist bobbed up and down. *Yes.*

The Colonel smiled and so did she. He showed her how to set up the mortar, attaching a tube to a baseplate and then extending the bipod. He made some figures on a piece of parchment, measuring the angle before setting it. "Driveway," he said, using the word they agreed would be the default.

"Driveway," she nodded, eyeing the adjustment knobs and matching them to the paper, hoping the Colonel got them right.

A few moments later Vince spoke into her ear, "This is Red leader. All teams report in."

The Colonel leaned forward, winked at Briaca, and dropped his voice an octave when he said, "Roger, Red leader. Red *One* standing by." He pointed at his eyes, then at the manor.

Briaca nodded and raised her binoculars.

"Red *Two,* standing by," Jake replied.

Paul added, "Red *Three,* standing by."

Vince whistled a series of chirps into his microphone then added, "Good. May the force be with you all."

This made the Colonel chuckle.

Vince waited several seconds before saying, "Let's do it, then. Red One, go on the first pyrotechnic."

One sentry walked the sidewalk above the house, pausing above the edge of a three-tiered waterfall to scan the property.

A bright light lit the horizon, then a twisting glow reached upward. It disappeared. Moments later a brilliant explosion of color began the display. Vince hadn't lied. The fireworks were magnificent, a fiery exhibit that drew every eye to the sky, even Briaca's for a moment.

But she had a job to do and forced them back into the binoculars, watching the sentry as he turned to face the lake. A muted shot left the Colonel's rifle and a spray of blood exploded from the sentry's head. His knees buckled and he fell across handrails and over the side of the waterfall.

Only then did the young woman realize what overwatch was really meant to do. She turned, terrified to face the killer of a man a furlong and half away, and watched as he calmly spoke. "Red Two, go," he said. "I repeat, go for alpha. Overwatch established."

She knew he meant the real fireworks had begun.

Jake and Lois moved up from the lake, disappearing into the trees for ten seconds. Briaca held her breath and waited. They reached the edge of the green lawn.

"Red Two at alpha. Overwatch one," Jake asked, "are we clear to advance?"

The Colonel replied, "Clear."

Through her binoculars she saw a man by the pool. She mercilessly slapped the man beside her, getting his attention, and pointed. He trained his rifle in that direction.

"Hold, Red Two! One is rounding the pool from west to east."

"Holding."

Briaca heard another muted shot and caught a whiff of the rifle's smoke. It would have been pleasing if this man had not just killed two men. *Not men. What am I doing?* She nearly forgot these were lesser vampure.

"Bullets... wyrcan," she said aloud in old Germanic, hoping the Colonel knew what she meant.

"Yes, it appears they *are* working," he whispered back. "If we get a headshot, at least."

"Red Two, approach the target," he said into the microphone.

"Break!" Vince said into everyone's ears. "Hold, Red Two. A vehicle is approaching the mansion."

Briaca turned to the Colonel who shrugged. This was unexpected. She raised her binoculars and scanned the property near the gate. A large SUV made its way down the lane, rolling slowly over the waterfall. Her heart pounded as she prayed no one would look down and see the body.

Two armed guards exited the manor and approached the driver. One of them was speaking into an earpiece of his own. He suddenly appeared worried, then stepped back to scan the property.

"He just realized one of his buddies is missing," the Colonel grumbled then pointed at the bag beside Briaca. "Make boom now," he said. "Driveway!"

She looked at it warily, this part scared her more than a bit. The SUV was in the middle of their default target zone. "Now?" she asked.

"Now!"

"Big boom or little boom?"

"Big... the biggest boom we got!"

The guard traced the steps of the first sentry, moving up the drive. The second still spoke to the driver. While the first neared the waterfall, Briaca pulled out what Vince had called a shell. She trembled but did not drop it until sliding it partially in the tube. As soon as it dropped she covered her ears and watched.

The shell left the tube with a whoosh, just as the guard had looked over the side and found the missing sentry. Before he could reach his hand to his ear and warn the others, the Colonel's gun went off and the man fell down, atop his friend. A heartbeat later, the SUV exploded in a fireball.

"What the hell, Colonel?" Vince complained. "We don't know *who* or what was in that vehicle!"

"Go Red Two," the Colonel commanded, ignoring Vince.

"Red Two moving," Jake transmitted. Briaca watched two figures race across the greenspace and up the path to the east entrance. "Breach."

Briaca watched as they simply opened doors and walked inside. "No visual," the Colonel advised the others.

The second guard, blown twenty paces from the vehicle, stood as if merely dazed. As soon as he took a step he fell to the ground in a heap. "Splash tango," Vince said into the radio. "Is Red Two inside?"

Briaca looked, they had entered the house. The Colonel radioed they were.

"Good, the house is clear except for the target. Red Three move in for backup."

"Roger," Paul confirmed, and two dark shapes raced along the green path from the event pavilion to the house.

Briaca watched them enter, wishing she could see inside, when Vince again interrupted. "We have trouble. Check the SUV." She watched as the windshield of the twisted vehicle kicked out from the inside. Six figures crawled out, unharmed by the explosion that would have certainly killed humans. They noticed the dead guard nearby, then sprinted for the house with inhuman speed.

"Both teams! Get out of there *now*!" Vince commanded.

"We can't," Paul replied, out of breath. "We've engaged thralls."

The Colonel sat up, quickly dismantling his rifle and pointing for Briaca to do the same with the mortar. They stowed these away as fast as they could. "Come," the man said, pointing to their rendez-vous point. It was time to move toward the water and ready the boat.

She nodded, looking down to grab her bag. As soon as her hand touched the handle she heard a muffled grunt. Turning, she saw three dark figures had tackled the Colonel, taking him to the ground. Two more stood beside Briaca.

She recognized them immediately as voltur, pale and malnour-ished, their skin stretched across their broad bones. They must have been hiding in the boathouse, alarmed and came out to investigate the explosion. She reached for her knife as they lunged. These crea-tures were fast but, luckily, Briaca was faster.

The new blade reflected no light, a dark iron with swirls from each time it was folded on the forge. Weaker than steel, these blades could be easily broken. The forge master had warned Vince the edge would not be as sharp. She didn't care about sharpness, or about strength, as she slashed it across the first voltur. She only cared that the dragon bone worked as well as it had in the bullets.

Do your thing, Argant, she thought as the edge traced a line across the creature's chest. It did more than sizzle. The wound smoldered as soon as it was created, quickly burning flesh in an outward spread as if fire had touched dry grass.

The creature howled from the pain, filled with lamentable torment as it's skin, bone, and organs beneath melted away. It collapsed on its knees and writhed with misery of death taking its time.

Nearby, the creatures atop the Colonel were trying to remove his bite collar. They paused, turning to watch, wide eyed and full of fear. This allowed him to get his own blade free, stabbing it in the side of one's neck.

As soon as Briaca's knife slashed for the other attacking her, it backed away, afraid of the iron in her hand. Again she proved faster, leaping like a wild animal attacking her prey. As it tumbled backward with her on top, she viciously went to work hacking until its head rolled down the hillside.

The Colonel had rolled free and the two remaining voltur now raced toward the house, out of reach of all but the man's rifle—and it rested in pieces inside its case.

The sound of gunfire came from the house and Vince spoke into everyone's ear. "I lost visual, I'm moving in to aid both teams! Red One, get the boat ready!"

"You've got two more creatures headed your way," the Colonel warned his friend. "Be careful!"

"Roger."

Briaca pointed at the Colonel. "You go, I fight."

"No. Vince said you aren't ready," he protested.

She pointed to the two burning voltur beside her and gave her new friend a wink and a smile. "*Mine* did not get away," she said in heavily accented English. She was picking it up so quickly.

The man stared back with a mixture of amusement and awe, then waved her off. "Go. I'll meet you at extraction."

Briaca pulled Kado's dragon tooth from her satchel then left her bags for the Colonel, eager to join the battle inside the house.

Chapter Eighteen

Briaca ran as fast as she could, leaping over rocks and bushes which would have so easily tangled or tripped a human in the dark. Her pulse raced even faster, switched on by combat. It somehow improved her vision, making the night as bright around her as day. Her other senses were also enhanced. She smelled the trail left by the voltur, a rotting stench left on the air, and her ears could hear the entire commotion within the house. She heard a nearby rattle, sensing movement. Everything moved in slow motion, even the snake spooked by her sudden arrival. As it struck she did too, swinging her dark blade and removing its head from body in midair.

The hybrid never missed a step in her stride.

That's what she had become, the form she had chosen, equal parts from each Keryx. Briaca had died beneath the bite of Lars, drained and replaced by something better. In her chrysalis vampure sanguis had mixed with Argant's, making his granddaughter nearly as much of a Keryx as he. *She* would control the vampiric urges and also the ways her body had changed.

She ripped off her shirt as she ran, stripping down to the black sports bra beneath, then gave in to Goro's final gift. She had earned it when feasting on Kado's blood, so pure, so intoxicating, it enhanced her form.

Lars had called her his Sigma at the cave, but she was not. Through her brother's blood, Briaca, daughter of Conrad, was already a Delta when Argant changed her fate.

The ridges pushed out against her cheeks, raising her brow. But the two spikes which pushed out from each temple were not of vampiric design. These rose up as magnificent horns, sharp and strong as the daughter of Oksana—descended from dragons. Sharp scales pushed from the skin along her spine, leading down her back as two large and leathery wings protruded from her shoulder blades. These beat against the air and lifted her high into the sky.

Briaca did not have time to sightsee on this maiden flight. She checked the watch on her arm, ignoring the explosive display all around her. Only ten minutes had passed since it began, still launching brilliant colors reflected in the lake. As she peered down at the villa, she became a true overwatch, viewing the battle raging beneath a dome of glass.

Inside, all four students fought valiantly against five voltur. Vince arrived at the same time as the other two, and a desperate fight ensued. The humans and their dragonkind professor were losing.

Both Vince and the Colonel had been wrong about Lars. He was not hiding in his panic room, recovering as if in a sarcophagus. He had met his vampure guests as they rushed in, alarmed by the explosion of their SUV. They, it appeared, were members of his massive legion.

Briaca watched as he stood beside two Epsilon and four Theta forms. All six dwarfed in the shadow of their Beta. Her friends could not fight this large an army alone, and she could do little against so many despite she was a strong Delta.

Raising the dragon's tooth to her lips, she blew a trumpeting note that echoed through the night, then dove. Only Lars recognized the horn, curiously looking upward as she crashed through the dome. Glass shattered and fell upon everyone inside, and Briaca pushed her full momentum into the chest of Lars. Together they tumbled and rolled into the bedroom.

Vince heard the glass shatter and instinctively covered his eyes. His first thought was that more vampure had arrived, not recognizing at first who had barreled into Lars. By the time he realized it was

Briaca, she was already fighting one on one with the vampure. He did not have time to marvel at her transformation and hoped she would remain on their side.

His second thought mourned his decision to lead his students into this danger, under informed and ill prepared. He quickly dispatched three voltur, taking advantage of the momentary distraction of most eyes marveling over Briaca. She was equal parts dragon and vampure. When he looked up from his kills, he realized Paul and Jake had also killed voltur, giving Daphne and Lois a fair matchup against theirs.

These new blades worked wonders, cleaving the skin of these creatures and leaving it to sizzle as if from dragonfire, ripping the beasts asunder from the inside out. Vince briefly watched their blood bubbling like acid in the rug. It was these blades which kept the six vampure at bay. They watched with interest, judging the efficacy of both the weapons and the skill of these humans.

He raised his shotgun, pointed it at nearest vampure, and blasted. The pellets worked nearly as well as the knives, and the full spread tore flesh from the Epsilon's face and ripped holes in his chest. But it did not kill him, only enraged both him and the others.

"Good gods!" the Colonel said into his earpiece. "Twenty more thralls just left the boathouse! Get out, Vince! They're headed your way!"

Twenty! Great Scott! Vince thought. "Which door?"

"East side!"

He moved beside his students, pumping shell after shell into the staggering vampure, covering their escape. "Fall back! Go out this door and get to extraction!" he told them. "I'll cover your retreat!" All four raced from the room just as his final shell ejected into the room. He could not hope to reload in the time it would take these creatures to reach him. It appeared they knew that as well.

The vampure lunged.

More glass abruptly shattered, this time from the large window behind the professor. A dragon's head roared angrily at the now stunned vampure. All six stood frozen by fear.

Another monstrous head reached through the ceiling, biting torsos off two, ripping apart the ceiling to get inside. This dragon only had one eye, the other covered by centuries of scaly growth to cover the hole where it should have been.

The monster behind Vince wriggled through the wall, stunningly magnificent as moonlight lit her blue and yellow scales. She was an aerouant, long and slender and almost snakelike as she slithered instead of lumbering like her larger friend. She too snapped, taking the head off the nearest vampure. The other three rushed into the bedroom, shutting the door behind them.

The dragons roared, tearing through the wall to reach the vampure locked inside. Heavy thuds on the roof announced the arrival of more dragons. These were lighter and sounded bipedal.

"Briaca," Vince warned into the radio, "you have more company." Three blasts from a shotgun meant she had dropped both her knife and dragon's tooth during combat. The professor prayed she had at least driven them first into Lars.

The blue and yellow aerouant snapped her head around, just noticing Vince, and growled. Her heat warmed his face but he smiled shyly without flinching. The shattering of glass from the next room suggested dragons made it inside.

The professor should have been terrified, but found himself mesmerized by the pools of fire that were her eyes. She could kill him any moment and he'd barely feel the crushing bite, but he somehow *knew* she was only judging him friend or foe. In usual Vince Redder fashion, he nervously cracked a joke.

"You're absolutely the most gorgeous dragon I've ever seen," he said. "We should hang out, sometime. You know, fly around, eat some Whataburger, maybe roast some vampires if we're feeling cute."

She cocked her head. Vince could swear she actually smiled before crashing through the wall. At least dragons thought he was funny, he wished he could say the same about his students. The creature left a hole large enough for him to watch the battle in the next room.

Briaca was fine, it seemed. As the dragons consumed the lesser vampure, Lars tried to flee. She caught him by the legs and dragged him down, holding the Delta while the aerouant carefully grabbed his upper body in her jowls. She held but did not bite down, leaving the killing honors to the hybrid.

Lars struggle but the dragon held. His body burned where the tips of her teeth had gently pierced skin. The pain was almost too much to bear, slow torture dragging out his pending death. The Salvator watched as Briaca dashed across the room to recover both her blade and the dragon's tooth.

She eyed each weapon as if unsure which to use.

"You hesitate to kill me?" Lars asked with a smile. His arrogant charm once again making him appear outwardly calm.

"I do," she replied.

"It's because you are drawn to me, just as I am to you. A legionary cannot kill their Salvator. Goro's blessing ensures that law remains followed. Go on, try," he coaxed, "you won't be able."

"Goro's *infection* no longer affects me. Argant neutralized it. Now I know it was only a virus, a presence in my blood which sickened me, but no longer. My body owns it now; my mind is in control."

"If that was true, you would not have chosen this form."

Briaca approached, sheathing her bone infused iron and gripped Argant's tooth tightly. "I could have chosen a dragon form, any one I wanted, but I'm not fully a dragon thanks to you. And because of the Ancient One I'm also no longer a vampure. Since I don't belong to either bloodline, yet possess the sanguis of both, I chose my *own* form, and will wear it proudly while killing every last one of your kind."

"Why the tooth?" Lars demanded with a frown. "Your new weapons work just as well."

She pressed it just below his sternum, pushing against but not breaking the skin.

"This belongs to my brother, Kado the Courageous, a hero greater even than Erwan the Bold. You were right when you said that legend is told wrong, full of lies told by arrogant dragons. It would lead one to believe Erwan was the prophesied vinculum, who will win the war over your kind. But Kado is that dragon walker, and the honor of fulfilling his vengeance belongs to him."

Lars grinned. "Go fetch him then."

"You once told me how much you enjoy sarcasm, but I despise it. I always preferred irony. Kado isn't here to complete the quest that led him to destiny, but he never would have fulfilled that prophecy had you not taken the one thing from him he loved more than dragons. Isn't it ironic that, through your attempts to turn *me* into one of your kind, you created Kado, the weapon who will kill Goro?"

"I remember that boy. He was pitifully weak and always scared. Goro will dispatch him easily the moment he shows his face."

Briaca went on, ignoring the threat. "He was a sweet boy, a bit bull-headed at times, but he never had a killer inside of him, not even after you destroyed the lives of those innocent people in Cardac. He does now, I'm sure, after your kind killed Mother."

"How do you know he won't blame and come after *you* for draining his father before his eyes?" Lars demanded, laughing despite the pain. "Your brother may not be a killer, but *you* are. I made you powerful, enough that you can resist me. But you *still* belong to Goro, and there's no resisting him. How about *that* for irony?"

Briaca smiled up into her Salvator's eyes. "That was my point," she said, her words dripping with sarcasm. "*You* turned me into the killer of *you!*" She pressed Argant's tooth slowly as Lars writhed, watching his heart burst into fire beneath his ribs.

This ended the monster who had raided Cardac, separated children from their mothers, killed helpless old men, then turned a girl into a mindless killer of her own family. As the festering wound burned outward, the aerouant let go. Both she and the hybrid watched Goro's prized Beta writhe in pain until his heart exploded.

"Hot damn!" Vince exclaimed. "They *can* be killed!"

Several sets of dragon eyes turned to face him, but so too did two swirling pools of blood. Whatever Briaca had become, she was no longer human.

Dregal stared down at Briaca, sniffing her closely, repulsed by the smell of vampure on her skin. It oozed from her, but she had worn it well along with her scales and set of dragon wings. It mattered that the stain was cured long ago by Argant. The microorganisms from Goro's saliva killed, but it still remained inside for him to sense.

He was the senior Elderkin now and did not want her in his presence. But he couldn't kill or force her into exile. He also could not ignore that she wore a disgusting form, not quite a dragon but neither so a vampure. She had proven herself worthy of his aid and had just enough dragon sanguis to be considered one of his thunder.

He snorted his disgust and swished his mighty tail, looking toward the sky and yearning to flee this place. Humans would arrive soon. He could already smell them approaching. The sound of sirens meant their police were coming closer.

The human beside Briaca, the one covered in the blood of the vampure and voltur he had killed, boldly stepped forward with the arrogance of a dragon. He was nearly too bold for his own good, but that only amused Dregal instead of offended.

"I am one of you, possessing a genetic kindred to dragons, but I'm afraid I don't know anything about our kind, especially how to properly thank you. At risk of insult, I simply say that I appreciate that you arrived when you did."

"The horn of Argant called us," the Elderkin explained, "a sound we know very well and will always defend." Dregal looked at the human more closely, frowning and inspecting what he found. What he discovered surprised the Ancient One, finding a human with enough dragon blood to almost deserve a different form. That transformation, if ever granted, would depend on his further worthiness.

"How are you called, dragon human?" Dregal demanded.

"I am Vincent, Vincent Redder."

"I did not ask your name, I asked how you are called. I see you are a warrior, but are you a king among these people?"

"Heavens no! I'm a professor, only a teacher of languages and history."

Dregal nodded. "Both are admirable studies, as important to *our* future as well as yours. If you ever need assistance, blow again on Argant's horn." With a soft roar he called the blue and yellow aerouant to his side. She landed softly, lighter on her feet than Dregal had ever managed. "Stay around this region, Parciel. Keep an eye on these hybrids and an ear out for their horn. If they need assistance, I want you to provide it. Watch this man dragon especially carefully." He pointed a claw at Vincent. "If you deem him worthy, then so too will I."

Parciel eyed the dragon human and nodded, leaping into the sky to join the thunder. Dregal, turning his back to the humans, followed.

Vince let out a held breath. "Well now, that was unexpected."

Briaca nodded, her body in the process of changing back to its human form. "You've met dragons now, and one of them is judging you."

"What do you mean *judging* me?"

"Parciel is deciding if she will accept you as her vinculum and, if she does, the vampure will always smell her on your skin. They will sense your bond and you won't be as hidden as you once were," Briaca warned.

"That's no problem. Dean Fields promised us better accommodations as soon as he can swing them. I'm going to propose something farther underground than our basement. He said he's got donors lining up to fund our endeavor, and I think we might even go national."

Briaca looked up and smiled. "You mean you want to go after Dominus Titus?"

"I mean exactly that. But it will be *President* Tito Morales we take down, and that'll be a tougher task than this."

They turned to watch the dragons fly off into the moonlight. The fireworks display had ended and police sirens now grew closer.

Vince pointed to his students by the water, collected in the boat. They were waving frantically, ready to shove off and race to their getaway cars on the other side. "I guess we've started something we have to keep doing?" he said as if asking Briaca's permission.

"I've got nothing else to do but learn better English and fighting, at least until my brother awakens in his new form."

Vince reached out at hand and Briaca took it, shaking their agreement. "Come on," he said. "I've got some things we can do until he's ready to join us. The first of which is get a good burger. I'm hungry, aren't you?"

Briaca realized she was.

"Come on," he said, jogging away. "Let's go grab some Whataburger! You like mustard?"

She had no idea what he was talking about, but food sounded good. She also noticed, for the first time in two thousand years, she hadn't thought about thirst.

Chapter Nineteen

Present Day

Briaca had done all she could for her brother. Kado slept soundly but would soon awaken. Dregal had told her he was ready. But the boy needed to hurry—a legion was on its way.

Soon she heard a tapping from inside and the chrysalis shook and rocked back and forth. The shell of it was still tough, possibly too much so for him to escape. Soon a small hole formed and an eye appeared. It *was* early. That eye was still protected by a scaly covering. Eventually, those would break off and blink away, discarded and unneeded by his new form. She hoped that would happen soon. He would be blind until it did.

The efforts of this struggle exhausted Kado, and he seemed to have passed out from the strain. *He needs his strength*, she knew, and waited patiently for several more minutes.

During this time, which felt like forever, her eyes kept darting to the passage behind her. The longer he took the sooner the enemy would find them. She had grown adept at fighting, but he would awaken vulnerable and weak. *Hurry!* she silently urged her brother. Thankfully, he did not sleep long.

After a few moments he began ripping away the broken pieces of his shell. He made an opening just big enough to slip out, naked and older, onto the rocky floor of the cavern.

Briaca stared down at Kado. The boy she once knew, the brother with whom she had been raised and raised herself, now wore a man's body. She knew this would happen, but was ill prepared for how much he resembled their father. She choked back a sob as her brother collapsed again from the effort.

Their father, once a simple dirt farmer named Conrad, had loved his wife and children. He did not deserve the end his daughter gave him. That Briaca would spend eternity looking upon her brother in Conrad's form was a penance. A punishment from the gods themselves.

Kado had rested long enough and they had to hurry.

"Wake up!" she shouted.

He stirred but it would be difficult to move fast after spending nearly two thousand years in that chrysalis. One thousand, six hundred and seventy-five, to be exact.

"I know it's early," she urged him, "but danger comes, and you won't be able to defend yourself."

Kado stretched, his muscles aching with cramps. He rolled onto his belly and tried to get up on all fours. His hands were still coated with the leftover yolk that should have nurtured him another five years or so. He slipped, his face landing hard against the stone, and blinked. His eyes were unseeing in the blackness, but his scales had begun to loosen. He tried to speak, but no words came.

"Easy now," she said more tenderly. "You've only just awakened, and your body has changed. It moves differently than it did before. Go slowly and let it adjust."

He put one hand against the ground followed by the other, wiping his palms before trying again to press up onto his knees. He drew in a deep breath before trying to stand.

"Hurry," she begged. "We cannot fight so many and must flee."

"Who..." The weak sound came out of his mouth full of uncertainty, testing the air around him while his mind struggled for words. "Who are you?" he asked.

She wanted to tell him everything but could not. The memories transferred from Argant to him must come slowly, or they would be tainted by whatever spin the vampure blood in her body gave him. To not even trust herself worried Briaca deeply and so she answered, "Who I am doesn't matter. Not yet. What matters is who *you* are. Do you remember anything at all?"

He said nothing, only stared into the darkness while trying to remember.

"What of the war?" she tried. "Do you remember why you transformed?"

"I... I don't even know who *I* am," the man whispered.

"That's normal," she promised. "When I awakened, I felt that way for several hours, with some memories not returning for weeks after. Even now, *years* later, I am still discovering the knowledge with which we were entrusted."

"Who are *you?*" he weakly demanded.

He doesn't recognize my voice!

"You will have to discover that in time, along with your own memories. Anything I tell you now may confuse facts as you once knew them. But I promise you will know all this and more very soon. Reach to your right," she told him, "and you will find a bucket of water and rags. Drink from it first, then use the rest to cleanse your body of the yolk."

He felt around and found the bucket. With trembling hands, he picked it up and brought the water to his lips. He drank deeply, then set it down and picked up the rags, dipped them in the water, and slowly washed his body down.

"After you are clean, feel to your left and find the clothing I laid out for you. It may seem strange at first but put it on the best you can. We can adjust it later."

He put down the rags and felt around the stone to his left. Several folded garments were placed in a pile, and he put them on in the order he found them. A t-shirt, a pair of jeans, and a hoodie. He touched the openings and guessed which part of his body on which to place them. The last items he found was a pair of leather boots. He pulled on the footwear.

"I'm sorry we have to move so soon before you're ready," she said, deeply worried about waking him so early, "but a battle is raging in the entrance to this cave." That had been a lie but not a big one. There was no battle, but the vampure and voltur *were* seeking him and would be watching the entrance. "We cannot leave that way, but I know of another."

She gently reached down and grabbed his hands, letting him feel her skin and squeeze them with wonder, then pulled him onto his feet. She helped steady him, then pressed a dagger into his palm, knowing he would not be able to use it, not yet, but felt better knowing he had it.

He squeezed it, seeing with his hands, then drew the iron from its leather case. Instinctively he tested its sharpness—a mistake given the soft state of his skin. A tiny trickle of blood ran down his hand. Dragon's blood.

Briaca felt a stirring, an insatiable thirst. She yearned so badly to give in, to end her brother's life now, to drink of his sanguis and be done with his presence entirely. She would choose another form...

"Careful!" she hissed, ripping lustful eyes away from the sight of his blood. "Tie it to your waist and let's be gone." As soon has he had tied the knot, she grabbed his unspoiled hand and dragged him away. "Don't worry," she said. "Your eyes will recover as well as your mind, faster even. By the time we reach the surface you will see clearly."

The tunnel she led him through grew lower. She warned him to duck. Soon it was so low they had to crawl on all fours. She led him with her voice, to a cool breeze and the soft sounds of nature near the opening.

Together, the pair approached the surface. Soft moonlight now lit their way. She glanced over her shoulder to see him better. His scales must have fallen off because he looked up at his sister, almost as if remembering.

At least he saw her.

She wanted to tell him everything. About Mother and Father and Argant and Lars. But she knew she could not. He had to remember on his own. The way he looked up at his sister unnerved her. Oh, that he would remain ignorant, both of her true nature and of what she had done to Father.

She managed to offer him a brief smile despite her worries. "We're almost there," she told him as the passage grew so that they could once more walk upright. "Keep your blade ready just in case."

"Just in case of what?" he asked.

He does not yet remember the face of his enemy. "You'll know them when you see them," she said.

"I think I somehow do, I just don't know the name for them," he admitted. Then, after a slight pause, he asked, "Is it *voltur?*"

"Very good," the woman said proudly. This time her smile lingered. "It won't be long until you fully remember your other form."

"Is that what I just did? I emerged from a cocoon?"

"In a way."

"What am I then?" he asked.

"You are what you chose," she replied curtly, "and I won't explain any more until you remember what I need you to on your own."

"Vampure," he said suddenly.

"Yes, those too," she agreed.

"There's one close by." It was an observation more than a warning.

"What?" The fact he knew or sensed voltur in her surged panic through her body. "Why did you say that?"

"I don't know, I just... I *feel* a presence that my mind faintly remembers."

"Well, you're wrong," she quickly snapped.

"So, we *can* feel them?" he asked. "I'm not imagining that feeling?"

"Of course not. What you're feeling must be confusion in your mind, memories mixing with imagination as the visions settle themselves out." She silently wished he would remain ignorant, never remembering what his sister had nearly become.

"So *you* can't feel them?" he asked.

Surely he isn't sensing me! she thought. "Don't be ridiculous." This wasn't a lie. Of all the knowledge she had acquired from Argant, no dragonkind had ever the ability to *sense* the vampurekind. "As great an ability that would be, no, we can't *feel* vampure presence, no more than they can sense *us.*"

But *she* could, because she was also one of them.

"Well, I swear I can," he pressed, but then dropped the issue.

Together they stepped out from the cave and into the night. Taking in a deep breath, they both let the cool air fill their lungs, replacing the mustiness of the cavern.

The land stretched out for many miles in all directions, mostly flat, but rugged and rocky. Off in the west and south, the land folded and rose into soft hills. This place, called Texas, differed in so many ways from their Switzerland.

"It's odd," the man said, "this place is so different than any vision I've seen since awakening. It's like I emerged on a different planet."

"Yes," the woman agreed. "I thought so, too, when I stepped outside."

"You hatched like I did?"

"I did, but there was no one to help me. I crawled out naked, terrified, and had to wander the caves alone until stumbling on a way out."

"Why?" Kado asked. "Why me? Why come back to help me, and how did you know I would hatch?"

"Awaken," she corrected. "Stop saying *hatch* like you were just born."

"Okay, how did you know I would awaken when I did?"

"You weren't supposed to, not yet. But I needed your help and so I hurried you along."

"Why? What's so dire that you woke me? Was it those creatures I imagined? Those voltur?"

"Yes, them *and* the vampure."

"What are they?"

"Look, I awakened you early, and I can't tell you anything about your past. You *have* to figure the details out on your own, or what I say can taint the truth you gained by the transformation."

He looked around. There were no voltur, none of the vampure either. Only miles of open land and a soft glow on the distant horizon. "What's that?" he asked. "Is something burning in that direction?"

"No. It's a city." She didn't need to look in the direction of Austin, her amazement had matched his when first laying eyes on it.

Kado looked at his sister again, taking in her face and pondering so deeply their connection. She wanted so badly to tell him, to admit *everything*. She knew then he would figure out the truth on his own.

He cocked his head as if listening to the night. His face changed, full of distrust and alarm. "Prove it," he suddenly said, setting his feet firmly on the ground and drawing his knife from its sheath.

"Prove *what*?" Briaca feigned, she knew what he was about to ask and eyed his blade nervously.

"Prove there is a battle. Take me to it and show me which side you fight for. Perhaps you are tricking me, fighting on the *other* side than my allies."

"Allies?" she decided to bluff and forced a fake laugh. "You have no allies here except *me*."

"Then who fights the battle?"

She paused, looking around. *Where the hell is Vince?* she wondered. He should have been here waiting. No problem. He could meet them along the way or she would walk her brother all the way to Austin. "This way," she finally said, pointing toward the glowing horizon.

"No." Kado abruptly turned, walking the opposite direction.

"Come back!" she hissed, afraid to raise her voice should the enemy be near. Her tone had stirred something inside. She realized too late she had spoken to him the way she did when he was a child, after Mother and Father had left, full of false authority.

He paused mid step. Slowly Kado turned, his eyes full of shock as dozens of memories flooded in at once. He stared at his sister, looked into eyes, his own full of overwhelming fear and experiences best forgotten. He was lost in the horrors of their childhood.

Behind her, a vehicle topped the ridge, kicking up a cloud of dirt as it approached. It was Vince, thank the gods, and his beloved Ford Bronco. The rocks his wheels sprayed stung her skin as he skidded to a stop. From inside he leaned over and pushed open the passenger door.

"Get in!" he cried. "They're coming!"

Briaca ignored him, turning to her brother in his state of catatonic remembrance. "You have to *help* me, Vince! He's remembering everything all at once!"

"Excellent timing," Vince muttered, climbing from the vehicle and hurrying to help. "Come on, kid," he urged. "It's gonna be a long night!"

Chapter Twenty

"Kado!" Briaca screamed into her brother's ear. "Can you hear me?" He had been this way for several minutes, with eyes open but seeing only memories left by Argant or reliving his own or someone else's past. His body seized and spasmed, his mouth foaming only slightly, as every muscle contracted.

"Damn it, brother!" she urged. "Shake loose of this quickly! We can't carry you and fight at the same time!"

The vehicle bounced and a voltur thumped against the roof. Vince spun his wheel, swerving and heading off in a new direction.

"How long will he be like this?" he asked.

"I don't know!" she snapped. "Kado, can you hear me?" Of course he couldn't answer, not yet. "He's burning up, like he has a fever," she observed.

"Did that happen to you?" Vince asked.

"No. My recollection wasn't anything like this at all." This too was something she hoped neither her brother nor Vince would learn, the dark secrets she must bear alone for the rest of her days. She thought again about that ancient struggle she had witnessed, how the Keryx had fought for control over humankind.

"Vampure," Kado whispered softly.

"Yes, Kado, and also voltur," she answered back, thankful he was coming to. The vehicle swerved again as it raced. It was time to begin explaining things to her brother. "They're attacking us *now* and we need you to come out of this trance!"

"I am Kado," he realized.

"Yes."

"And you are Briaca."

"Bingo!" Vince shouted in that annoying way he often did. "Ding, ding, ding! Winner, winner, chicken dinner!"

Kado blinked his eyes, the visions faded but not completely evaporated from his mind. "What is this vehicle?" he asked, running his hand along the leather interior.

Vince took his eyes off the road and grinned behind his silly mustache. "A 1986 Bronco, the most badass SUV ever made. With a three-inch suspension lift, two inches of body, and..."

Briaca cut him off, pointing a finger toward the road. "Vince! Shut up and drive!"

"How does it move without horses?" Kado asked.

"Oh, it's got plenty of horses under the hood, a 5.8 Windsor V8!" Vince replied, swerving to ram a vampure swooping down from the sky. He hit it directly, crushing the creature's chest against the heavy brush guard. It slid off quickly and disappeared beneath the vehicle. Both right wheels bounced over its body with resounding thuds.

Briaca rolled her eyes. "Vince," she said, "he *just* awoke. The first thing he learns about this century shouldn't be about cars!"

Vince shrugged. "Fine, I'll teach him about the culinary treats of our century. Let's shake these things and stop at Round Rock. I'll get him some Whataburger. You like mustard, kid?" He swerved again, striking down two more voltur.

Kado stared up at his sister. "Where is Argant?" he demanded.

Argant. She too wished to have found him upon awakening, and did in a way. Briaca touched the bundle on the floorboards. That was all they had left of him, the weapons made from his bones. She would save that for later. "He died so that we would transform. He's nothing more than bones now."

"These memories, everything flashing behind my eyes, these are his."

"Yes, his and all that were passed down to him."

"You've seen them too?"

"I have." Briaca lied. She had only seen bits and pieces from the *wrong* perspective.

Kado stared up into her eyes, his finally focusing. Then he shuddered. *He knows now.* That shudder meant he had noticed. He reached up and touched her cheek, forcing a smile of his own. "You chose your form," he said softly, "as did I."

Tears trickled down Briaca's cheeks and she stifled a sob. *Could it be that he understands?* she wondered, nodding affirmation to his realization. "We are fighting a war, brother, one we're currently losing."

"Is that why you awakened me early?"

"Yes. We need your help. Nearly all the dragons are gone."

"If they're gone, what are we fighting for?"

Briaca stole a glance at Vince, driving the vehicle. He hadn't swerved in some time and seemed to have relaxed behind the wheel. "We're fighting now for humans, and for Argant's bloodline... *our* bloodline."

Kado sat up, taking everything in—Briaca, Vince, the Bronco, even the clothes they all wore. He peered outside the window and watched the world blur past him. His face, now older and so much like Father's, stared back as his reflection. He reached up and touched the glass. "I look like Father."

He abruptly stiffened, reaching up to touch a spot on his neck, the side Briaca had bitten. He remembered *everything* now.

Briaca placed a hand on her brother's shoulder, but he pulled away instinctually. "It wasn't me," she tried to explain, but it was too soon for him despite how many years had passed for her.

"I know it wasn't," he agreed, "yet it *was* at the same time. Are we like *them* now?" he asked.

"No."

"But your eyes are just like theirs."

"Only at night. It actually helps me walk among them when I choose, just as Argant promised." Argant had promised them many things would happen if they accepted this form, had sworn they would become something quite remarkable. They would be dragon walkers, but the venom of the vampure still swam in their veins.

Hopefully, Kado would never know his sister's blood thirst.

"And mine?" he asked, meaning his eyes. The reflective lights of the city had made it difficult to see the color of his own in the glass.

Briaca leaned forward, reaching over the seats, and grabbed a visor hanging above the passenger side. With a tug she ripped it free.

"Hey!" Vince protested. "I'm gonna need that!"

"Shush," she scolded the driver who went on muttering about how the angle of the sun would someday blindly run him off the road. She held up the visor, the center of which had a tiny mirror.

Kado saw clearly his own face. His eyes, burning like two pools of fire, swirled and danced like those of dragonkind.

"You're him," Briaca said. "You *are* the dragon walker."

A loud popping sound followed by a terrible shaking and thumping echoed from the road as both front tires blew out. The Bronco abruptly screeched to slow its momentum, swerving and squealing as it came to an abrupt stop.

"Hey guys," Vince called, pulling a black object from a compartment near his side, "we've got company." Fifty voltur encircled the vehicle, closing in on it slowly.

"Are you ready?" Briaca asked. "Have you the strength to fight?"

"I don't know how," Kado replied honestly.

"Then stay in the car," Briaca said with a wink, "and I'll teach you later." She pulled a bundle out from under her seat, a wrapped bundle of linen. She quickly uncovered the object within.

Kado recognized the dragon's tooth at once.

Briaca and Vince threw open their doors and stepped out of the Bronco, leaving Kado safely shut inside. Together the pair stood back to back, Vince with his shotgun and her with her Taurus Judge. Briaca also wielded the dragon's tooth with her left. She held it to her lips and blew a long note that echoed across the prairie. As she pulled it down, she smiled at the enemies now rushing toward her.

The deafening blast of buckshot filled the night, flashing brightly and illuminating the battlefield like strobes. They dropped several voltur immediately, tossing them backward from the concussive blasts. Both Briaca and Vince fired again and again into the advancing horde until the monsters came too close to range down. They quickly holstered their guns and drew blades—short, dark swords that refused to reflect the moonlight above.

The fight that ensued blurred with inhuman speed as the voltur dashed around, biting and clawing at the pair. Though Briaca was noticeably faster than Vince, both matched speed with the creatures, striking out with overwhelming strength. The man used the hilt of his sword to land a blow across the chin of one, sending it spinning away and crashing to the ground. With a single slice he brought down the blade, severing its head from its shoulders.

The fight lasted only a few minutes before a heavy crash shook the field.

Dregal and his thunder had arrived. He, Parciel, and their wyverns rushed from their landings, ripping into the voltur and scattering them in every direction. Soon others arrived, five more wyvern who flanked their master as three aerouants cut off the now retreating voltur. In a matter of minutes, none of the demons survived.

Kado fumbled with the door handle and pushed it open, stepping into the night. He ran straight for Dregal.

The massive beast turned, snapping at the man running toward him before cocking an angry head. Two streams of dragonfire illuminated the battlefield, reflecting a grisly scene. Two swirling pools of fire watched Kado approach.

Dregal gave a huff then snorted the fire out quickly. "So you survived the transformation, it seems."

"Yes," Kado agreed.

"Then it's time you stopped being a man and become the dragon inside of you." Dregal turned toward Briaca. "Train him, teach him these new ways and make him ready. War is coming, and it's time we *all* came out of hiding to fight it."

She nodded. "I will, Ancient One."

Turning back toward Kado, Dregal added, "I was against this, what Argant proposed. But he was right. The time of our kind has passed, and this world belongs to man now. It's too late for me, but our offspring will have a chance to share this world. We need those like Vincent who can walk among humans and live like them." He cocked his head toward Briaca and let out a rumbling growl of disapproval. "We also need abominations like you and your sister, it seems." With a great beating of wings, he rose into the sky, circled once, then headed off to the west. His thunder followed.

Once they were alone, Kado eyed Vince carefully. To any human the man appeared normal, no different than any other mortal. Other than his inhuman strength and lightning speed, there was nothing else out of the ordinary.

"Look closer, Kado," Briaca urged quietly. "Remember that sense you felt when we were in the caverns? When you sensed a vampure but none were about?"

"Yes, and I still sense that stain though all these are dead."

"You sensed *me* brother. I am the hybrid, but I am more their kind than dragon. You bonded with Mother, and that kept your blood pure. She protected you from the virus Lars injected into you. That's why she died, Kado. Mother died saving *you* from this curse while Father's death strengthened it within me. Oh, brother, please forgive me."

Kado reached out, hugging her closely, and wept, finally mourning what they lost nearly two thousand years earlier. After a long embrace they pulled away and Briaca pointed toward Vince.

"Look at him," she said. "See him with that feeling in your blood. Use that ability to examine this man, to see him for his bloodline instead of with your eyes."

Kado took a deep breath and closed his eyes. Finally, he understood, just as Argant the Storyteller, had sensed his grandchild before he even knew of his lineage. That was why he had taken a special interest in the boy, setting all of this into motion.

The dragon walker opened his eyes and saw the man as Briaca did, with fresher clarity. Gone were Vince's human qualities. His eyes held the slightest bit of fire behind two dark irises, hidden from all except another of his kind. His skin, though outwardly human, was comprised of tiny scales interwoven and sprouting hair as if he were a mammal instead of reptilian. In his chest, a heart beat warm blooded but the blood it pumped flowed with sanguis, that nectar of a dragon's soul that clearly distinguished it from humans.

"Hi, cousin," Vince finally said to break the tension. He gave Kado a wink and holstered his black sword.

"Is that iron?" Kado asked, pointing at its hilt.

"Not entirely." Vince looked toward Briaca as if hoping she would explain. She did not. It wasn't time. With a shrug he pointed toward the Bronco. "Come on," he said. "You also get to learn how to change a tire. The sun's going to be up soon, so those things won't return. But Austin is about forty miles away and I'm starving. I want to get these changed out so we can get home."

Briaca still watched her brother when he turned, and they both remembered a time, long ago, when a bossy older sister sent her petulant little brother out into the rain for firewood. She wanted so badly to apologize for how she had treated him, for all of the arguments and wasted words they could never get back. She had been afraid, a mere girl left alone to raise a man. It wasn't fair to her, the unbearable weight of responsibility, but she had never realized how unfair it also was to him. She should have been more empathic, more loving and nurturing.

"We're not part of the thunder, are we?" he finally asked.

"No, and we never will be. Not with Dregal in charge."

"Then I guess we are back to where we were before."

"What do you mean?" she asked, confused. Were they never to have a relationship now. Was it too late for them as siblings?

"We only have each other, sister." He reached out and hugged her closely, squeezing his sister tightly.

She hugged him back, crying tears of both regret and hope upon his shoulder. No matter what danger tried to split them, or what crazy old man promised adventure, Kado and Briaca would never choose anyone or anything else over family.

Loved this tale?

Don't miss the story of Kado!

Now read these events from his point of view. Experience more adventure while discovering Dragon Legends!

Books by T.B. Phillips

Dragon Thirst
Legends (September 2023)
Mythos (September 2023)

Andalon Saga

Andalon Origins
Andalon Project (April 2022)
Andalon Paradox (April 2023)
Andalon Prophecies (Expected Winter 2023)

Dreamers of Andalon
Andalon Awakens (June 2019)
Andalon Arises (July 2020)
Andalon Attacks (December 2020)

Children of Andalon
Andalon Legacy (September 2022)

Corrupted Realms
Orphan Knight (July 2023)
Wailing Tempest (May 2021)
Howling Shadow (September 2021)

Chilling Tales
Ferryman (October 2022)

Corrupted Realms
Orphan Knight (July 2023)
Wailing Tempest (April 2021)
Howling Shadow (September 2021)